ERIN ENTRADA KELLY

The Land of Forgotten Girls

SCHOLASTIC INC.

ISBN 978-1-338-11051-7

Text copyright © 2016 by Erin Entrada Kelly. All rights reserved. Published by Scholastic Inc., 557 Broadway, New York, NY 10012, by arrangement with Greenwillow Books, an imprint of HarperCollins Publishers. SCHOLASTIC and associated logos are trademarks and/or registered trademarks of Scholastic Inc.

12 11 10 9 8 7 6 5 4 3 2 1   16 17 18 19 20 21

Printed in the U.S.A.   40

First Scholastic printing, October 2016

The text of this book is set in Berkeley.
Book design by Sylvie Le Floc'h
Calligraphy on p. 214 © 2016 by Cindy Pon

To my sister

❊ 1 ❊

Ghost

Sometimes I stare into the dark corner of my bedroom and see the ghost of my sister Amelia. She's ten years old—the age she would be now, if she hadn't died—but she doesn't talk like a ten-year-old. She has the eyes of a grandmother and the voice of a saint. She's raven haired. Her skin is like cream. The perfect color skin, people always said.

"You sure have made a mess of things," she says, and then she disappears.

After she leaves, the room is quiet except for the steady breathing of my youngest sister, Dominga—who everyone calls Ming—and the sound of the rats in the walls of Magnolia Tower, which is the name of the apartment building where we live. I've never seen a single magnolia on my street and it's not much of a tower. Maybe the people who built it thought we wouldn't notice, so long as it had a good name.

Magnolia Tower is in the town of Giverny, Louisiana. You've probably never heard of Giverny, since no one wants to come here. I sure didn't. But this is where we came to live after my mother died and my father married Vea.

She married him for his papers, the ones that would take him from the Philippines to America. Everyone knew it, even him. But he didn't care. He didn't know anything about raising little girls, and Vea was the first woman wearing red lipstick to walk up to him at my mother's funeral.

"So sorry about Mei-Mei, falling sick that way,"

said Vea. But something in her voice told me she wasn't sorry at all. And I didn't like how she made it sound like getting sick was my mother's decision. "They say cancer, but I say broken heart," she continued. "Must have been hard for her after little Amelia died. She was such a beautiful little girl."

Vea looked right at me when she said it. I was standing there, grim faced, with Ming on my hip.

"Now what you going to do, Juan?" she said to my father. "You can't go to America with two little girls all by yourself."

"We're going to live with Auntie Jove," I said, maybe because I was little and didn't know any better. But I assumed it to be true. The sky is blue. The trees are green. And Mama had a sister who would take care of us. I couldn't imagine me and Ming being raised by our father—Vea was right about that. But as soon as the words leaped out of my mouth, I knew I was wrong.

Vea's eyebrows shot up. She looked from me to my father.

"I didn't know Mei-Mei had a sister," said Vea.

My father glared down at me. Was he sad or mad or both?

"She doesn't," he said.

"Yes, she does," I said. "Mama told me all about her. She has a sister named Jovelyn who rides elephants and goes on adventures in the Sahara Desert and travels to faraway places like India and Macedonia."

She has a blond streak in her hair from the time she was blessed by fairies. She climbs mountains and flies airplanes. She's the most beautiful woman in the room, any room, and the cleverest, too. That's why no one ever sees her. She moves so fast and is so busy with adventures that she never stays in one place long. She can have any prince she wants, but she doesn't want one. She is much too busy. That's why she's even better than Cinderella or Snow White. My mother said so. My mother said.

"She doesn't," my father repeated.

Behind him, a solemn crowd was slowly

approaching, ready to say how sorry they were that my mother had died. What a tragedy, they would say, again and again. Poor Juan—he lost a daughter one year before and now he'd lost his wife. But Vea didn't move right away to make room for the others. Instead, she blinked at my father and smiled.

"So sad," she said. "What a terrible thing to happen just before you were going to leave for the States." She brushed a painted fingernail against my father's cheek before she walked away.

When she was gone, I looked up at my father and said, "Mama had a sister. She told me so." Ming squirmed in my arms and buried her head in my neck.

"Those were fairy tales, Sol," he said, eyes focused straight ahead. "You'll live a better life if you ignore made-up stories and focus only on things you know to be true."

❧ 2 ❧

The Land of Giverny

Things I know to be true: Tita Vea married my father so she could come to the States, and there is nothing magical about that. And there is nothing magical about Giverny, either, even though it's just outside of New Orleans and people say New Orleans is loud and fun and *vibrant*. Giverny must have drained from its gutters.

We live on the ground floor, in apartment four. There are sixteen apartments in the Tower, and there is nothing magical about apartment four. There is nothing special about any of them, actually. Vea says they're all alike: each one has a living room; two small, square bedrooms; one cramped bathroom; and a kitchen with three cabinets. On each floor there is a hallway right down the middle that's either too dark or too bright. When it's too bright, the light bulb makes a buzzing sound and you can see all the water stains in the ceiling, but when it's too dark, it feels like you're walking into a horror movie. Our apartment is at the end of the hallway right next to a broken elevator and a dark stairway that looks like it leads to certain doom.

The only nice things in our apartment are the four plants that sit under the window in the living room. The window isn't very big, so the plants are gathered up together to get the most sun they can. The plants are my favorite things in the apartment, but they belong to Vea so I don't let on how much I like them.

The apartments in the Tower are considered

"affordable housing." There's a big sign on the side of the building that says so. I didn't always know what that meant. At first I thought it meant that you get all the furniture in the apartment, because when we moved, the furniture was already there and it didn't even belong to us. And then I thought maybe "affordable housing" meant that you only get really terrible furniture, since ours had stuffing jutting out from the cushions, and all of the legs on the coffee table were wobbly. But pretty soon I learned that "affordable housing" just means that you don't have much money.

After one week of living in apartment four, I walked up to my father as he cooked *pancit* in the kitchen and said, "Papa, can I ask you a question?"

He sighed. He didn't like questions. Finally, he said, "Yes, Sol?"

"If we don't like it here, can we send the papers back and go home?"

Instead of answering, he just sighed again.

That was a long time ago. I'm twelve now, Ming

is six, and we are still in apartment four. We still have the wobbly furniture. And the rats in the walls. The only thing we don't have is Papa. Three years ago he went to the Philippines for his father's funeral and he never came back—so I guess the answer to my question was yes, but only for him.

Unfortunately, we still have Vea.

"You will call me Mother," she said soon after we moved to apartment four, back when Papa was still around—even though he was never really around much. When she said this, Ming and I were sitting on the couch and Vea was standing over us, smoking a cigarette. She didn't even flick the ashes into an ashtray; she just let the ashes fall onto the carpet and then she'd rub them in with her foot.

Ming blinked at her.

I said, "No, I won't."

Vea grinned. "You will, Soledad."

"I won't."

I'm not a disobedient girl, even though Papa and

Vea say I am. Vea thinks it's because I'm being raised in America, but that's not it. I just don't think it's right to obey orders that you know are wrong—and calling Vea "Mother" was as bad as cursing God. I would take five years off my life before I would ever call Vea "Mother" because she was so unlike my real mother that it was hard to believe my papa ever wanted to marry her in the first place. My mother's skin was soft, like a pillow. Vea's is rough, like sandpaper. My mother liked to make up stories and fairy tales. Vea likes to tell us that we're too fat, or too skinny, or too disobedient. Vea smokes cigarettes until the countertops in the kitchen turned yellow. My mother put flowers behind her ear.

"You're a bad girl, Sol," said Vea. "And do you know what happens to bad girls?"

"No," I said. I smiled. "Please, tell me. Do they get ice cream and cake? Do they get to take rides in a long limousine? Tell me, Tita *Vea*—what happens to bad little girls?"

✖ 3 ✖
Figs

If you want to know what happens to bad girls who
live with an evil stepmother, I'll tell you: they get
put in the closet. You've probably heard that before.
But when you are the daughter of Mei-Mei Madrid,
closets are of no concern to you because a closet can
become anything. Your mind is a palace. That's what
my mama used to say. So the first time Vea sent me to
the closet, I pretended I was inside a rocket, the kind
that they launch into space. When Vea took the chair

away from the doorknob and released me, I stayed in for an extra fifteen minutes, until Ming opened the door and stuck her head inside.

"Why haven't you come out?" she asked.

"I'm not sure if the atmosphere is safe," I said. "What is your world like, Earthling?"

Ming looked around the inside of the closet—at the bent hangers, beat-up shoes, and dusty toys— and then raised her eyebrows at me. "Huh?"

"I have been transported into space. You are the first being I have seen in thirty-two years. Tell me, what is your planet like?"

Ming turned around and looked at our bedroom. Then she scratched behind her ear and said, "It's kinda messy."

I nodded, came out, and pretended to be an explorer. As I was exploring the marker stain in the comforter, Ming asked me if I was going to call Vea "Mother" from now on.

"Never," I said.

"Me neither," said Ming. "Not even if she locks me in the closet forever."

"That would never happen."

"Why?"

"Because if she ever hurt you, I would cast an evil spell on her that would turn her blind and deaf and then she could never find you."

Not only did Ming refuse to call Vea "Mother," she quit talking altogether. Not completely, but she hardly ever speaks to Vea at all anymore. She talks to me, though. Sometimes too much. Mostly she asks questions.

I remember one time last summer she practically grilled me about Amelia, which is one of my least favorite things to talk about.

It was hot that day, and we had to wear long sleeves because we were picking figs. If you don't wear long sleeves when you pick figs, your arms get itchy.

"Why did Amelia go in the river if she didn't know how to swim?" asked Ming. She was only one year old when Amelia died.

"She was little. She didn't know any better," I said. I felt something turn in my belly. It's that feeling you get when you think of something terrible at an unexpected moment. I'd only been thinking of figs, not about my dead sister. But when Ming said her name, something turned.

I was seven when Amelia drowned, but I remember like it was yesterday. I wish I could forget. I wish I was like Ming, too young to remember what it was like to have another sister. But then I wouldn't be able to remember my mother, either, and no wish is worth that.

"Why wasn't Mama watching her closely?" asked Ming. "I thought real moms always watch closely."

I tied my hair into a knot and pressed my lips together tight.

"Let's talk about something else," I said. I reached for a branch and held it down so she could pick the fruit. "Let's play I Spy."

Ming picked a fig and brought it to Mr. Elephant's

stitched mouth. Mr. Elephant is her favorite stuffed animal. My father gave him to her right before we left the Philippines. Even though his name is Mr. Elephant, he's actually a purple giraffe.

She eyed the tree trunk and said, "I spy something brown."

Ming would make a terrible spy.

When I didn't guess right away, she looked up at me. "Do you know what it is?"

"Yes. It's the biggest broomstick ever made. Big enough for five witches."

Ming looked around for the broomstick, then said, "No, Sol. It's the tree trunk."

I gave the tree a pat. "This? Well, *this* is what I was talking about in the first place. All the witches have to do is come down, pull it out of the ground, and take off. They'll probably be here any minute."

Ming sighed and rolled her eyes, as if I was the most immature playmate she'd ever had. Then she took a big breath of air and hurled Mr. Elephant's fig as far as she could. It landed just a few feet away.

"Did Mama have any sisters?" she asked.

The back of my neck dripped with sweat.

"She used to tell me she had a sister named Jovelyn," I said, flatly. Suddenly I didn't feel like picking figs anymore. "She called her 'Auntie Jove.'"

Ming's eyes lit up like coins. "Really?"

I hadn't thought of Auntie Jove in a while. Her name felt familiar but strange all at the same time. Once I started talking about her, I couldn't stop. I told Ming all about Auntie Jove's adventures, and how I thought we would live with Auntie Jove after our mother died, but instead our father married Vea and brought us to Giverny. The fig tree didn't offer much shade, but the more I talked and watched Ming's eyes light up, the less I noticed the heat. When I finished, Ming was quiet for a moment. Then she kissed Mr. Elephant's head.

"Too bad you don't have any sisters, Mr. Elephant," she said.

"Mr. Elephant doesn't need sisters," I said. "He has you." I grabbed one of the branches and shook.

"Everyone needs sisters!" she said as the figs fell at her feet.

❧ 4 ❧
Snap

When you live in Magnolia Tower with lots of large families, you hear all kinds of sounds during the day—mysterious bumps, furniture scraping against the floor, cabinets opening and closing, faucets turning on and off.

But at night, you hear the rats.

Rats make scurrying sounds when they move. They always seem to be in a big hurry. I hear their little feet, mostly at night when everything is quiet.

Scratch and patter, scratch and patter. There's no other sound like it.

We hardly ever see the rats because they only like to move around when the lights are off and it's dark outside. Vea says they're only in the walls. I wonder what it's like to live inside walls, scratching and pattering in complete darkness. It makes me shiver just thinking about it.

The rats are worst when it's cold, but I can hear them now, even in the summer, as I lie next to Ming in our bed. School is out and in thirty minutes it will be midnight—the first official day of summer break.

"What are you gonna do this summer?" asked Ming. Mr. Elephant was nestled into the tight crook of her arm.

"Don't know. What about you?"

"I'm going to work on some art pieces. Miss Paulsen said I was the best artist in the whole school. She even gave me a set of special pencils. She told me not to tell anyone because she's not supposed to

show preferential treatment, so don't say anything."
She paused. "Sol?"

"Yeah?"

"I hear the scratching sound. Do you?" She
snuggled closer to me.

"Yes."

"Do you think the traps will get them?"

Ming didn't like the idea of rats scratching around
in our walls, but she *really* didn't like the idea of them
getting clobbered by traps. When she saw Mr. Bowman,
the superintendent of our building, laying the traps one
afternoon, she followed him around our floor, asking
how the traps worked and if they hurt. The super
finally told her to leave him alone. She couldn't sleep
that entire night because she was waiting to hear a snap.

"No," I said. "They're protected by the Pumpkin
King who also lives in our walls. He makes sure they
don't get whacked by the traps."

"Can he also make sure *we* don't get whacked? By
the rats, I mean."

"He can do anything. That's why he's the king."

I closed my eyes and thought of the long summer stretching in front of me. I was so tired, I felt like I could sleep for twenty years. Summer break couldn't have come fast enough.

"Sol?" Ming said again.

"Yes?"

"Do you think we'll have a good summer?"

"Yeah, sure. Why not." I was too tired to sound convincing.

She was quiet, but I knew she had more to say. I could tell.

"Last week I made it to the tree house at school before anyone else when the bell rang for recess," she said. "No one saw me—not even Miss Paulsen—so I yanked up the ladder and kept it inside with me so no one else could use it. I sat way, way in the corner so they couldn't see me. I had recess all to myself." She paused. "Do you think you and Manny could build a tree house for me tomorrow?"

Manny is my best friend. His real name is Emanuel Esposito.

"I don't know anything about tree houses," I said. "And I'm pretty sure Manny would nail his fingers together."

"Could you try, at least?"

I yawned. "I've never built anything. You have to know how to do that kind of stuff."

"I bet it's not that hard."

"That's what you think."

"But maybe you could just try. It doesn't even have to be a big tree house. It could be a small one."

"Go to sleep, Ming. It's vacation."

"Will you just *try*, though? You and Manny could—"

"I don't know anything about stupid, dumb tree houses, Ming," I snapped. "Ask someone else."

I regretted it as soon as the words left my mouth. She didn't have anyone else to ask, and I knew it.

"I guess I'll stay home, then, even though it's the first day of summer," Ming said, quietly. "I'll probably just work on my pieces or write another letter to Auntie Jove."

My eyes flew open, like I'd just been bolted with electricity.

"Write a letter to *who*?"

"Auntie Jove."

I hadn't heard that name since the day we picked figs.

"How could you write a letter to Auntie Jove when . . ."

"When what?"

When she doesn't exist. ". . . when you don't have her address?"

I imagined her writing to Auntie Jove the same way she wrote to Santa Claus—sealing a letter, writing "Auntie Jove, Philippines" on the envelope, and dropping it in the mailbox for a confused mailman to find.

"I found Papa's letter and asked them to get the address. That's how."

My father wrote us one letter after he left for the Philippines. It was only four sentences long. *Dear Sol and Ming, I hope you are doing well. I'll be home soon. Be good for Tita Vea.* He mailed it from a relative's house—a distant relative that we'd never met, whose address we didn't recognize. We have many of those.

"Papa's family doesn't know her," I said.

My mother once told me that she didn't want my father to meet Auntie Jove. *She is so beautiful that men fall in love with her on the spot! They say Helen of Troy had a face that could launch a thousand ships. Well, Auntie Jove's could launch two thousand! And everywhere she goes, she takes the scent of freshly bloomed roses with her.*

"I know. I explained all that in my letter," said Ming. "I asked them to find her for me and give her my letter. I haven't heard back yet."

The air around us was suddenly heavy. I thought of her at that mailbox again. I wanted to hug her and tell her that it was all made-up. There was no Auntie Jove. It was just a story.

"Sol?" Ming said.

"Yeah?"

"What does 'preferential treatment' mean?"

"It means when you like one person more than another, even though you're not supposed to, so you treat them better."

Even though it was dark, I could tell she was smiling.

"Miss Paulsen is my favorite teacher," she said, then she turned over with Mr. Elephant.

Two minutes ago I was so tired I could have fallen asleep in seconds. Now I was wide awake. Ming had written a letter to our father's family. What did it say? Did she mention Vea, or just Auntie Jove? Had it even reached anyone? The way I remembered it, the return address wasn't very detailed. I even wondered at one time if it was real, or if he made it up, the same way he made up that he was coming home "soon."

As soon as I heard Ming's sleepy breathing, I stared into the dark corner and waited.

Amelia would appear and tell me what to do. It had always been that way. The first time she came out of the corner was in our house in the Philippines, after our mother died. I told Amelia how sad I was and that I hoped they were together somewhere. I told her I was scared because now it was just me and Ming, and my papa didn't seem to have any idea what to do. And I told her I was sorry that she died and that maybe Vea was right—maybe our mama died of a broken heart because Amelia was perfect and she loved her so, so much. I talked and talked until Amelia told me to go to sleep, which I did.

From then on, Amelia was there. She'd step out of the corner like a guardian angel—just like she was doing now.

Her eyes appeared first—light and wise. I always thought she would have turned out to be the smartest one of the sisters, if she hadn't died.

Then her white skin and black hair.

"She thinks Auntie Jove is real," I whispered.

"Why didn't you tell her the truth?" Amelia asked.

"She has to believe in something. Everyone has to believe in something."

She rested her hand against her milky cheek.

"I believe in the truth," she said, and then she was gone.

✖ 5 ✖

The Chinese Phantom

Things I know to be true: Manny is never on time. If he says he's going to be at the Tower at nine in the morning, he'll show up at fifteen minutes before ten. That's why I was still sitting on the couch watching TV when Vea came home from her job at the Stop-N-Go. Sometimes she works the midnight shift and she gets home when everyone else in the Tower is waking up. A plastic Stop-N-Go bag dangled from her wrist. Even from the couch, I could tell that it held a carton of cigarettes and a Styrofoam box of greasy fried food. The Stop-N-Go serves things like fried chicken, popcorn shrimp, and deep-battered catfish, and they keep it under this lamp that makes it look like the food is in surgery. At the end of the shift they give Vea the leftovers and make a batch of fresh food, which is still gross, only not as greasy. When Vea's in a good mood—which is, like, never— she brings home extra tartar sauce for Ming.

Today wasn't a tartar sauce day.

"That bat-crazy penny-pincher is standing in the front doorway again staring into space," she said as she walked in. She was talking about Mrs. Yeung, our neighbor who never speaks. "That old lady should be in a home. Maybe if she had family she would be. Imagine, a Chinese living alone. Most of the time you can't split them apart."

Vea never called our neighbors by their names. Instead she said things like "the Chinese" or—if they were alone—"a Chinese."

I wonder what our neighbors call us. I have a few choice names for Vea, but I keep them to myself.

". . . and she can afford to stay in a home, you know," continued Vea from the kitchen. She put the carton of cigarettes in the freezer. "She has a safe full of money in that apartment of hers. They have all the money. The Chinese are taking over our country."

Everyone on our floor is Chinese, except for us. Mrs. Yeung is in apartment three. The Kwoks are in apartment one, and the Langs are in apartment two. The Kwoks and Langs have lots of kids and adults living in their apartments, but they never speak to us. We only hear them. They're the ones who are always turning on the faucets, closing the doors, and slamming the cabinets. A bunch of the Langs work at the casino, which makes Vea angry because that's where she wants to work. She says the reason she can't get a job there is because they only want to hire the Chinese because they're good at math.

"It doesn't look like they're taking over anything

to me," I said. "Looks like they're all crammed up in apartments. If they want to take over America, they're not doing a good job."

Vea poked her head out of the kitchen and glared at me.

"When I said 'our country,' I was talking about the Philippines, you ignorant little *kano*," she said.

She filled her watering pail with water. "That crazy old bat owned a grocery store in the Philippines. Or at least her husband did, before he died," she said, walking to the window. She got on her knees, poured a small bit of water into one of the plants, and inspected its leaves. "They owned stores here, too. Made so much money, you wouldn't even be able to count it. But they stuffed it all in a safe. That shows she's crazy." She tapped her temple with her left index finger, then watered another plant. "They were lucky—never had children—so why do they need to keep all their money locked up? And then come to live in a place like this, just to shove it in our faces! I hear she has ten thousand dollars in there. She'd be lucky not to get robbed."

"Doesn't seem like she's shoving anything in our faces," I said. "Seems like she's got nothing."

"Things aren't always what they seem." She watered another plant.

"That sounds made up. I don't think she really has a safe full of money."

"That's what your father told me." She stood. Droplets of water fell from the pail as she walked back to the kitchen. "Then again, your father was a dirty liar."

She might have said more, except that's when Manny knocked on the door. Vea didn't make a move to open it, even though the door was *right there*. It's probably for the best, though. Manny's scared of Vea. He doesn't admit it, but I can tell.

I couldn't get off the couch fast enough. I stepped into the hall without saying good-bye. Manny was wearing his New Orleans Saints cap and his face was shiny. He must've run from his house because he knew he was late and I'd give him a hard time. He smelled like sweat.

"I'm on time," he said.

"No, you're not. You're forty-five minutes late."

"Same thing."

The hallway lights were off because it was bright outside and sunlight came in through the windows. One of the Langs—a mean-faced woman who always had her hair in a tight, tight bun—was at the row of dented mailboxes in the lobby. She was banging on the number two box and swearing in English. I bet her key got stuck. That happens a lot.

She didn't pay attention to us when we walked by. Neither did Mrs. Yeung, who was standing just outside the door on the stoop. She was staring off into space, just like Vea said. She does that sometimes. And when you pass by, she doesn't even smile or wave or say hello.

Today Mrs. Yeung was wearing thin white pants

and an oversized white shirt. She was so skinny that it looked like someone had draped the clothes over her when she wasn't paying attention. She was like a phantom.

Manny and I stopped talking as we got closer. Mrs. Yeung's silence has a way of being contagious. She stepped slightly to the side to make room for us to pass. She glanced at us briefly with dark, dark eyes. I smiled, just a little, just in case.

She didn't smile back.

⚜ 6 ⚜

The Snout

Once upon a time, there was a guy named Bishop Something Strout. He did a bunch of good stuff for Catholics in New Orleans—or maybe just Louisiana in general, or maybe just somewhere in the United States of America—and so they built a fancy school with a bell tower and named it after him. It cost a million dollars to go to school there. Maybe not that much, but a lot. The girls and boys who go there wear blue and green uniforms. Just about all of the kids are white.

If you want to know where the magnolia trees are, they're lined up right in front of the Bishop Strout School, which is nowhere near Magnolia Tower.

In addition to being forced to wear uniforms, there are two other not-so-great things about being a student at the Bishop Strout School: the kids from my public school, William Leonard Middle—Leo, for short—call your school "the Snout," and you get out of school for summer two days after everyone else in the district.

Every year since fourth grade Manny and I have taken advantage of this by terrorizing the Snout kids before their summer break. In particular, this girl with a red backpack who looks about our age. Her hair is white. It's so white it doesn't even look real. And her skin is like that, too. She looks like a ghost that's come to life. That's why we call her Casper. Manny says she's albino. Even that word is weird—*albino*.

Manny and I don't even know her; we just see her around town sometimes. She's hard to overlook.

We've always had a good time making fun of the Snout kids, with their freshly pressed uniforms and shiny black shoes. And it's not like the Snout kids don't pick on us. At the football games they scrunch their faces at us; some of them even pinch their noses, like we stink. So don't feel bad for Casper. We give her a hard time now and then, but she gets to go home to her big house and sweet parents. Manny goes home to a dad who works as a gardener— barely making enough money to keep the lights on (and sometimes those lights go off)—and I have to go home to Vea. I bet the Snout girls never had a mother and sister die, or had their fathers abandon them. They don't have evil stepmothers.

The albino girl immediately glanced at the magnolia tree when she crossed the yard.

"Look, look," said Manny, bumping my arm and tossing his hair out of his eyes. "There she is."

For no particular reason I'd been collecting acorns. I straightened up, tossed the acorns in the grass, and called out, "Hey, Casper!"

She looked at the ground and walked faster.

"Hey, don't miss your class now, Casper!" yelled Manny. He snatched up a handful of my discarded acorns and tossed one at her. She blocked it with her shoulder but didn't stop walking.

I grabbed an acorn and threw it. When it hit her on the head, Manny burst out laughing.

"Catholic skirts mean bigger flirts!" he yelled. That was one of his favorites. Some of the other Snout girls looked our way. They never noticed when we hollered at Casper, but they always looked when we said something that could be about them.

A few of them giggled, until Manny asked if they wanted to skip class and join us instead.

It's not the most amazing way to kick off summer break, but it's something.

"I wonder if Casper's ever been kissed," said

Manny as we walked away from the Snout and down Piedmont Avenue.

Piedmont Avenue has big, old houses with pointed roofs and green lawns with bright flowers. There are barking German shepherds behind straight wooden fences and sparkling cars parked in rows. Piedmont Avenue is about as different from my neighborhood as my mother is from Vea.

"Probably not," I said.

It was a sunny day and the birds were chirping really loudly. I love the way the birds sound, but I would never tell Manny that. He'd probably laugh.

When we got to the corner and crossed the street, he said, "Have you?"

I shoved my hands in my pockets. "Have I what?"

"Have you ever been kissed?"

"No."

"Why not?"

"What do you mean, why not?"

"You're—uh—pretty. You know, kinda pretty,

anyway." He cleared his throat. "I mean, you've got that long black hair and you've got this really, um, pretty face, too, you know? My dad says Filipino girls are the prettiest girls in the world."

I couldn't believe what I was hearing. I started laughing, like he'd told the biggest joke in history. I'd never heard Manny talk about any girls being pretty, much less Filipino girls.

He shoved me lightly into one of those neatly trimmed yards and said, "Forget it, forget it."

"Sorry, Manny. I wasn't laughing at you, I just . . . I don't know." I got myself together and said, "Besides, don't you think I'd tell you?"

"Tell me what?"

"If I'd ever been kissed."

He shrugged. "I guess."

"I mean, you're my best friend, right?"

"Yeah."

We crossed another street. The blue roof of Tippet's Grocery Store came into view a few blocks up. Tippet's is kind of a landmark in Giverny. Not because it's historic or anything and not because it's a fantastic grocery store—in fact, there's nothing fantastic about it—but because it sits on the curve of Eleventh Street, which separates the north part of Giverny from the south. In Giverny, people ask if you live south of Tippet's or north of Tippet's. People like Casper live north. Manny and I were headed south.

The chirping birds weren't as loud anymore because there are fewer trees the closer you get to Tippet's.

"You'd tell me if you kissed someone, right?" I asked.

Manny shrugged again. "Well . . ."

I stopped walking and crossed my arms. He stopped walking, too. The ends of his long hair were pointed with sweat. It was a really hot day. Sometimes it feels like there's no other kind of day in Louisiana.

"Wait a minute, Manny Esposito," I said. "Are you telling me that you kissed someone?"

"More like *someones*."

My mouth dropped open.

"Well, what do you expect?" said Manny. He started walking again. "We're not kids anymore."

"I know, but . . ."

"But what?"

". . . I just thought that you would have told me about your first kiss."

"I couldn't wait for you forever," he mumbled.

"What?" I said, even though I was pretty sure I'd heard him.

"Nothing."

We walked in silence until we reached Tippet's, then I said, "I guess I just don't care about kissing anyone, that's all. There are so many other things to do."

"Ha!" Manny poked me in the ribs. "Like what, Sol?"

He said that all the way back to Magnolia Tower, over and over again, "Like what, Sol? Like what?" He sounded just like one of those chirping birds.

7

Melting

Our bathroom mirror is small, square, and hanging sideways off its hinges. There's a little crack in the corner, which meant someone had been given seven years of bad luck. Maybe it was me and I just forgot that I broke it.

When I look into the bathroom mirror, this is what I see: A bad luck crack and a girl with a flat nose, dark eyes, black hair that's pulled in a messy ponytail on top of her head, lips that sometimes get chapped because she forgets to use ChapStick, a round face, and the shoulders of a boy. My skin is dark, much darker than Amelia's. When Amelia was a little girl people always said, *Oh, how beautiful! Look at her white skin! She has the face of an angel!* No one ever said those things to me. I looked more like my father, and people said he had the skin of a man who worked in the fields.

Maybe that's why I started laughing when Manny said I was "pretty, kind of." Amelia had been the pretty one, not me.

When I got home from the first official day of summer with Manny, I stood in front of the bathroom mirror with the door closed. I studied my face from all angles. Maybe I *was* pretty. I couldn't be sure, because I wasn't sure what "pretty" really meant. This would have been a good question for my mother. Or maybe my father.

Vea knocked on the door. "What you doing in there?" she asked.

"I'm using the bathroom!" I said sharply. "What do you think?"

"You been in there too long. Get out. They called me for another shift and I want to take a shower."

I glared at the chipped paint on the bathroom door and said, "I'll come out when I'm good and ready."

There was a pause before I saw the shadows of her feet move away and the sound of her slippers shuffling against the floor. She wears these slippers all the time and she doesn't pick up her feet when she walks. *Shlip-shlip-shlip-shlip.* It's the most disgusting sound in the world.

I turned so my back was facing the mirror and then whipped around really fast to look at my reflection. I wanted to see myself the way other people saw me. It's hard to tell what you look like to other people, so I tried to imagine that I was a complete stranger and seeing myself for the first time, but the more and more I looked in the mirror, the more and more

I just saw myself, Soledad Elia Madrid. I stared at Soledad Elia Madrid until I heard the *shlip-shlip-shlip* sound again, followed by a loud *snap* and *crack*—the sound of my evil stepmother kicking the door open with her grubby pink slipper.

She liked to kick things, so I wasn't all that surprised that she kicked the door open, but I wasn't prepared for the noise, so I stumbled backward and watched the lock dangle from the new split in the wood. I also wasn't prepared for what came next: being soaked with ice-cold water from Vea's plastic watering pail. At first it felt like my body was being stabbed by shards of ice, but it was so hot out that after a few seconds, the biting cold water didn't feel so bad.

Vea tossed the pail aside. It rattled in the corner while I stood up straight and twisted water out of my ponytail.

"You look just like a wet dog," said Vea.

I shook the water off my hands.

"*Salamat*," I said, which means "thank you."
"Same to you."

Vea's face twisted up, which meant she was getting ready to grab my nose. And that's exactly what she did: she snatched my nose between her thumb and index finger, squeezed it tight until my eyes watered, and pushed me backward. I would have stumbled over the toilet, but then she grabbed and turned my ear as she led me out of the bathroom. Once she'd pushed me into the hallway, she slammed the door, only the door wouldn't close all the way, since she'd broken the lock.

I wiggled my nose around to get rid of the throbbing pain, knowing it wouldn't do any good, then I touched the inside of both nostrils to see if there was any lasting injury. There wasn't. She's only made my nose bleed once.

I walked toward the closet at the end of the hall where we kept the extra towels, but once I saw the towels sitting in there, lined up in a neatly folded row—thanks to Ming, who has a strange need to keep certain things orderly, like her towels and her shoes—I closed the door again and walked into the living room, dripping wet. The relief I felt from the cool water was fading and now I shivered, but instead of changing, I sat on the living room sofa and opened the book that I'd left on the coffee table a few days before. I concentrated as hard as I could to stop myself from shaking.

By the time Ming came in the front door, holding Mr. Elephant, I had goose bumps all over my body.

"Did you just get out of the shower?" she asked.

I didn't look up from my book. "Kind of."

"Why didn't you dry off?"

"Each droplet is filled with magical powers," I said, surprised at the shakiness of my voice. I even *sounded* cold. "If I dry myself off, I will no longer be able to fly or read minds. And I need to be able to use my telepathic powers if I'm ever going to conquer the—"

The bathroom door wobbled open and Vea emerged. Ming closed her mouth into a tight line.

"Big *kano* and little *kano,* eh?" said Vea. She looked at me. "Dry off. You're getting the sofa wet."

"*You're* getting the sofa wet," I said. I was still reading my book, even though I wasn't really reading it. I was just staring at the sentence "He saw a flash of light, like a small rainbow, hovering at the edge." "Since *you're* the one who poured water on me."

Vea lit a cigarette and crossed her arms. "Do you want me to dry you off, then? I will dry you until your skin is raw. I will dry you until your bones snap." She lifted her hand in front of her face and snapped her fingers—*snap, snap, snap.*

Ming tapped my shoulder and nodded toward the hallway, which meant she wanted us to go to our room.

"Yes, go run to your room, you dirty little rats," Vea said.

And we did.

❌ ❌ ❌

The day after my papa applied for his work papers to America, my mother took two chairs from our breakfast table and set one in front of the other. After they were lined up, she told me to sit in the second chair with Amelia in my lap. My mother sat in front—her belly big and round, because she was pregnant with Ming—and asked, "Ready, *naka*?"

"Ready for what?" I said, adjusting Amelia's bottom on top of my skinny legs.

She looked at me over her shoulder. "For our journey to America, of course." She pretended to hoist a sail. She looked at the hard, dirt floor and said to watch out for dolphins and sharks. All around us, our imaginary world turned to water as we made our way east.

"*Dalayegon sa Diyos*! Good-bye, Philippines!" Mama said, waving good-bye to the rocking chair in the corner. I waved, too. I even lifted Amelia's pudgy hand and had her wave good-bye. Good-bye, bamboo mat. Good-bye, coconut trees. Good-bye, rocking chair. "We promise not to write!"

Every time my mother talked about us coming to America, her voice was full of pride, like we'd won the lottery. But when Vea talks about America, her words sound like thorns. It doesn't make sense to me, since Vea was so desperate to come to Giverny that she married my dad. But then again, Vea always talks in thorns. *Kano* means *American*, but the way she says it makes it sound like a bad word, like she's saying "cockroach" or "spider."

One of my biggest worries is that one of Vea's thorns will stick Ming and never get unstuck. After I got soaked with the water, Ming was quieter than usual, and I was worried this was one of those times.

When I asked her what was wrong, she said she was keeping a secret.

"Well, what is it?" I asked. She was sitting next to me on the bed with Mr. Elephant in her lap.

"I can't tell you. It's a secret."

"Is it a good secret or a bad secret?"

"I can't tell you." She smiled wide. Like I said, she'd be a terrible spy.

I hadn't seen her smile like that in a long time, not since she was a little girl, really, not since before we came to Giverny.

"Is it about school?"

She shook her head.

"Is it about Miss Paulsen?"

"No."

"Is it about your summer?"

She shrugged. "Maybe."

I rolled my eyes and flopped backward on the bed. "Whatever, Ming. I don't feel like playing kid games. If you want to tell me your secret, you can tell me whenever you're ready."

She fell back next to me and sat Mr. Elephant on her flat chest. "Does your nose hurt?"

"No," I said. It was a lie. My nose hurt pretty bad, but I knew it would go away by morning.

I read my book while Ming stared at the ceiling.

After a few quiet minutes, she said, "Sol?"

I sighed—just like my father used to sigh when I'd interrupt him.

"Yes?" I said.

"If we poured water on Vea, do you think she'd melt?"

I laughed. "Probably."

I stood up next to the bed, put my hands on my cheeks, and cried, "I'm melting! I'm melting! Oh, what a cruel, cruel world!" And then, with the sound of my little sister's giggles egging me on, I melted right down into the hard floor.

❊ 8 ❊
Stealthy

Things I know to be true: It's easy to steal ice cream from Tippet's.

The cashiers can't see the freezer from their registers and even if they could, they probably wouldn't watch it. There are three cashiers and they usually spend their time talking. Sometimes they talk to each other; other times they talk to the customers. Tippet's is a neighborhood store, so everyone knows everyone. Even Manny and me. I know that the cashier at register one is Imani, the cashier at register two is Maria, and register three is Raven. I like the name Raven. It'd be nice to be named after a bird, like you can fly away any minute. My mama once said she named me Soledad because it means "sun" and I was destined to brighten the world. Sometimes I wish she'd never told me that. It makes me sad for some reason.

Even though Raven has the best name, she's the meanest cashier. Imani and Maria laugh and joke around a lot, but Raven usually stands there with her mouth in a knot, complaining about how hot it is outside or how she doesn't get paid enough or how her boyfriend might be cheating on her with the neighbor. Vea said Raven "can't help being lazy," but I don't know why she thinks she can judge. When she isn't at Stop-N-Go, all she does is take care of her plants, watch television, and talk to her family on the phone. I used to eavesdrop on her conversations, hoping that she was talking to my father or making plans to find a better home for us, but she usually just talks about how she would send us back if she wouldn't lose the subsidy. I don't know what a subsidy is. Probably something important she gets that she doesn't share with us.

Because the cashiers are busy talking and the freezer isn't in their line of view, Manny and I usually swipe bomb pops like they belong to us. Then we walk down one of the aisles that doesn't have a camera pointed on it, pushing the ice cream into our pockets. It's so cold that it numbs my hip, but it's worth it. You have to move fast so they don't melt.

The day after Vea almost twisted off my nose, Manny and I got pops from Tippet's and sat on the milk crates stacked outside the store, facing the alley.

There's nothing better than ice-cold bomb pops on hot summer days. The chilliness made my nose hurt where Vea had twisted it, but I didn't care. I ate my bomb pop until red juice dripped down my chin and I had to keep wiping it with the back of my hand.

As we sat there, I told Manny about Mrs. Yeung's safe. His eyes widened.

"Maybe we should slip through her living room window one night like cat burglars and carry it out. Then we'd be rich and we could run off to the Bahamas or something," said Manny.

"No way," I said. "There's nothing worse than a thief." Manny and I figured the bomb pops didn't count. They didn't really belong to anyone. Just the store. "Remember Diego?"

Diego was a kid who went to our school for half of sixth grade. On the second day of school he stole Manny's favorite sneakers, the ones that Manny had begged and begged his father to buy for him. Manny cried that day, but I promised I would never tell anyone. I never have.

"Yeah, yeah," Manny mumbled. He didn't like to be reminded of Diego—not because Diego stole his sneakers and Manny got a whipping for it, but because he knows that I saw him cry. "I wonder how much money is in there."

"Thousands, maybe," I said. "Could you imagine having thousands of dollars and just living in that apartment building? I tell you what, if I had thousands of dollars, I wouldn't be living there. I would take the first plane out."

"To where?"

"I don't know. Somewhere."

"Yeah, me too."

Manny went to work on his bomb pop. He liked to eat it superfast, like he was racing the sun. When he was done, he threw his stick in the grass and stuck out his tongue. It was bright red.

"You look like you have a bloody mouth." I took the last bite of mine.

"So do you." He smiled. "You wanna kiss me while my tongue is nice and cold?"

I rolled my eyes. "No."

"Why not? The score is seven to zero."

"There's no *score*, dummy. It's not even a fair competition. When you kiss seven girls, everyone thinks you're a *babaero*. If I kiss seven boys, everyone'll start talking bad about me."

"Not me." He smiled wider. Parts of his teeth were bright red, too. "What's a *babaero*, anyway?"

I got down from the milk crate and tossed my stick into the grass next to his.

"It's a boy who kisses seven girls and doesn't even remember their names the next day."

I walked away from Tippet's, down Eleventh Street. Manny followed.

"I remember all their names," he said.

"Good for you."

"You're just jealous, anyway."

"I have other things to think about that don't involve your tongue in my mouth."

"Oh, yeah? Like what?"

I stretched my arms up to the sun and listened to the chirping birds.

"None of your business," I said.

We walked together like that for about half a block, each in our own thoughts. I wondered if Manny was thinking about all the girls he kissed, but then he asked if I really thought there were thousands of dollars in Mrs. Yeung's safe.

I shrugged. "Maybe." I narrowed my eyes at him. He didn't look very menacing with those bright red lips, but I sensed that he had mischief on his mind. "Why?"

"What if we snuck in there one night and looked for it?"

"Are you crazy?"

"What's the worst that could happen?"

I counted off on my fingers: "We could get caught. She could call the police. We could be arrested. We could get sent to juvenile prison—or maybe even adult prison. We could—"

"Okay, okay. I get it."

"Besides," I said, kicking a pinecone into the

street. "There's no way we could pull it off."

He scoffed. "Speak for yourself."

"What's that supposed to mean?"

"I have my ways."

"What ways? So in addition to being a secret *babaero*, you're a secret cat burglar, too?"

"No. But I know how to do it." He wiped his mouth with the back of his hand. The sun was beating down hard now. We were both sweating. Sometimes I wished I lived somewhere cold, like the Arctic, where I would never have to sweat my face off.

"You know how to do what, exactly?"

"Be stealthy. I heard all about it."

"From who?"

"Around."

That means he heard it from one of his cousins. They're in and out of trouble all the time.

"And what did they say?"

"First off, you need a plan. Almost like a map, so you know exactly what you're gonna do when you get in there. Like, first I'm gonna hit the bedroom, then the bathroom, or whatever. Then, once it's go time, you should dress in black so you blend in with the dark." He jumped up to snatch a low-hanging branch from a tree. It snapped off in one swipe, so he used it like a cane, sticking its ragged end in the parched grass. "Once you're all dressed and you've got your plan all mapped out, you go inside. But you can't walk like you normally do. That would just be stupid. You've got to walk on your toes first, then ease back on your heels. Or start with your heel first and ease onto your toes." He tossed the branch aside, stopped, and demonstrated. "That way, you don't make any noise." Once he was finished with his demonstration, we continued walking. "Don't turn on any lights— that's a 'duh'—even if you're in another room and you don't think anyone will notice."

"And what are you supposed to do if you get caught?"

He pulled at his earlobe. "You've gotta be listening

at all times. Like, on high-high alert. And if you hear something, you stop where you are and stand very still. Never take off running or anything stupid like that. You only move if you're able to hide. And then you've gotta do that heel thing with your foot so you're not clomping around like a horse. You've also got to be super-careful when you open doors. Turn the handle slowly and apply pressure with your free hand where the door meets the doorframe. Push a little, real gently, before you open it so it doesn't make any noise at all."

"Sounds like you've got it all figured out." I paused. "But we're not breaking into Mrs. Yeung's apartment to find her safe."

"Maybe not. But you never know when you might need to go into stealth mode. You know what I mean, Sol? You know? Huh? Huh?"

There he goes again, sounding just like a bird.

❧ 9 ❧

Princesses

Once upon a time there were two sister princesses who lived in a tower. They ate leftover gas station food, stale cereal, and peanut butter sandwiches—only they had to settle for creamy because the evil stepmother didn't like crunchy. They got five dollars a week to stay out of the stepmother's hair, but they managed to irritate her anyway. They did not get to take showers or baths every day because it wastes too much water. They didn't get to run the air conditioner during the summer unless it was an emergency, and it never was. The older girl got secondhand clothes from the thrift shop, which she passed on to the younger girl, even though the clothes were too big for her.

The girls once lived on a beautiful island surrounded by crystal water. All of the children on the island were like them, and all of them were happy. Then the girls were taken away from the island and locked in a tower where they now live with that evil stepmother. Down the hall is a rich woman with no family who keeps all her money locked in a safe. If she gave the princesses even one handful, they might be able to break free forever. But instead she guards her riches like a watchdog behind her sealed door. On the other side of town is a girl with bright white hair who lives in a house made of gold. She has no problems.

"There," said Manny as Casper emerged once again from the art building. Manny cupped his hand around his mouth and yelled, "Last day of school for you, Sister Saint! You wanna come celebrate with me?" He made a disgusting wagging motion with his tongue, but she ignored him.

"What you gonna do this summer?" I called to her. "Go to church and pray for regular clothes?"

Manny and I laughed.

I picked up an acorn, but then tossed it away and snatched up a pinecone instead. I don't know why. I wasn't thinking about the differences between acorns and pinecones. I was just looking for something to throw. So before I could even think about how heavy and sharp a pinecone could be, I threw it as hard as I could. It slammed Casper in the side of the face. This time, she couldn't ignore it. She immediately dropped her bag and put her hand over her eye. Manny was just about to howl with laughter, but when he saw her clutching her face, he stopped. So did I. So did some of the girls walking nearby. They went up to Casper and pulled at her wrist, trying to get her to show them the injury. When she did, Manny and I saw a trail of blood, but not much else. It was hard to see with all the girls crowded around.

"She's bleeding!" one of them said.

The trickle of blood looked dark and deadly against the pale white of her skin.

Manny and I had the same idea at the exact same time: *Run*. We turned and ran off the Snout campus so fast that I tripped over a big crack in the sidewalk. I heard someone yell out, "Hey! Hey!"—at least I think I did—but I regained my balance and didn't stop. Go, go, go. I tried not to think of the blood on Casper's skin or the way the pinecone felt in the palm of my hand just before I threw it. Instead, I thought about how fast I could get away from the Snout. Did you know there's more than one way to run? Running to get away is the worst kind. Every nerve in my body tingled with heat and fear. Every thought I had was *run, run, run*.

Manny was quicker—he breezed past with his chin up and his dark hair flying, calling out, "Hurry, Sol, hurry!" And I did. I sprinted after Manny all the way to Eleventh Street.

Once we were in the parking lot at Tippet's, we stopped to catch our breath. Sweat dribbled down my face, even into my ears.

"Do you think I hurt her?" I asked, through gasps.

"Well, she's bleeding. So probably."

"What if I blinded her or something?"

"It's not like she's gonna *die*." Manny stood up, still breathing hard. "I'm sure you didn't blind her. Maybe hurt her, but that's it."

"Thanks a lot. You're a big help."

"Don't mention it," he said.

Once we could breathe again, we started the slow walk back to our neighborhood. Neither of us talked much.

"What do you wanna do for the rest of the day?" Manny asked when we reached the Tower.

"Nothing," I said. "I think I'm gonna go inside and check on Ming."

Manny shrugged. "Okay, then."

The Espositos live about two blocks down the street, in a house with a shaky front porch, chipped teal paint, and two cars parked out front in overgrown grass. Manny started walking in that direction, but before he got too far, I called out his name and he turned around.

I wanted to ask him if he thought I'd hurt Casper real bad. If he thought maybe she was bleeding to death in the schoolyard on her last day of school. If he thought she would have to get stitches and have a scar.

Instead, I just waved him away, said, "Never mind," and stepped into the Tower.

❧ 10 ❧

The Legend of Auntie Jove

You may have heard the legends of Bigfoot and the Loch Ness Monster. You've probably been told stories about magical mermaids, centaurs, flying horses, and unicorns. But now let me tell you about another legend: the legend of Auntie Jove.

The first time my mother told me about Auntie Jove, we were walking near the river on our way to the market, just like we did every week. Ming was still a baby then; my mother carried her in a homemade sling on her chest. Amelia was four, and I was barely six.

"Slow down, *anak*," my mother called behind me. I was far ahead of her, stepping around rocks on the bank. I stopped, turned, and shaded my eyes. My mother moved slowly because of Ming, and because she had to hold Amelia's hand. I would've held Amelia's hand for her, but she never walked fast enough for me.

Once they caught up, I walked alongside them. Even though Amelia was four, she was quiet as a mouse and only walked and listened. She was the most well-behaved little girl my mother had ever seen. That's what Mama used to say. She would joke that God had given her two very different girls— me, who never stopped moving or asking questions; and Amelia, a fair-skinned girl who only listened. *I wonder how our Ming will turn out*, my mother would say. But she didn't live long enough to find out.

"Tell me a story," I said.

"What kind of story would you like, *anak*?" Mama

asked. "An adventure story or a fairy tale story?"

"Any kind."

She paused and looked at the river. "Okay. I will tell you a story about my sister Jovelyn."

"You have a sister?" All I knew were my uncles and I didn't really know them, since they didn't come around that much.

"Yes. She's much older than me. She's like a secret sister."

"Why is she a secret sister?" I asked.

"Because she *is* a secret. She's never even met your papa. She has a different mother than me and she was raised way up, up in the enchanted jungle, where magical things happen. She was raised by one-eyed giants and three-headed snakes, but she was never afraid because she was a friend to all. If I had been born in the enchanted jungle, maybe I would be off in the world, too. But I'm happy to be here, with my girls." She kissed Amelia's hand and the top of Ming's head.

"Does she have kids, too?" I asked. "Kids that I can play with?"

"Oh, no. Not Jovelyn. She never married. She's too busy on grand adventures."

"Like what?"

"Swinging from ropes in the rain forests of Central America and riding in elephant parades with pharaohs. She has even hugged the necks of giraffes!"

My eyes got really wide at the idea of an elephant parade.

The next time we went to the market, my mother told more stories. Auntie Jove took jet planes into the clouds, my mother said. She climbed the tallest mountain in the Philippines. She shook hands with the emperor of China; she stood on a stage with the president of the United States; she wrote books; she went swimming in Niagara Falls; she had a romance with an American movie star and a wealthy Venezuelan; she danced with a member of the British royalty.

I remember I asked my mother why Auntie Jove

didn't send us money, since she seemed to have a lot of it for her travels.

"She isn't rich," my mother corrected. "She's clever. That means she knows how to use her imagination. When you can do that, you can do anything."

"Maybe one day she'll write to us and send us pictures," I said.

"Maybe. If she's not in a faraway land."

It seems stupid now that I ever thought Auntie Jove was a real person who could send letters. If she could dance with kings and ride elephants, surely she could mail a letter, right? There was a time I thought so.

And now it was someone else's time.

Ming.

When I walked into our bedroom—still sweaty from my escape—Ming was halfway under the bed. Her two brown legs stuck out like skinny toothpicks.

"What are you doing?" I asked.

"I'm locking away my letter from Auntie Jove so you can't get it."

"Letter from Auntie Jove? What are you talking about?"

When she came out smiling, I sat on the bed and frowned at her.

"She wrote me back, Sol!" said Ming. "That was my secret."

I narrowed my eyes and said again, "What are you talking about?"

"I told you. She wrote me back."

I shoved my hand, palm up, in her direction. "Show me."

"No. It's my most prized possession and I'm never letting anyone see it. Not even you. I'll tell you what she said, though."

"Ming." I rubbed my temples. Thinking about Casper's bloody forehead and Ming's ridiculous letters was almost too much for my brain. "I need to see it, because if you really got a letter, there's no way it's from Auntie Jove."

Ming's smile disappeared. "It *is* from Auntie Jove, Sol."

I put my hand out again. "Let me see it, then. Just to make sure."

"No."

"No?"

She crossed her skinny arms. "I don't need to prove it to you. I know the truth and that's what matters."

"If you got a letter, it's not from Auntie Jove," I said. "It's not real."

A terrible thought occurred to me: What if someone in the Philippines really did get Ming's letter, and they decided to play a trick on her? Or what if it was someone right here in the neighborhood? What if they wrote to Ming and told her to meet them at a certain place and time? The so-called letter could be from anyone. It could be from Blackbeard, the evil junkyard keeper up the block who never smiled and kept a pellet gun in his overalls. There were rumors that he lured children into his trailer so he could starve and eat them.

"I knew you would say that," said Ming. "That's why I don't want to show it to you."

"Well, the only way to prove it's not made up is to show me the letter."

"You know what your problem is? You don't believe anything."

"Ming, if you got a letter from Auntie Jove, it might be someone playing a trick on you. Someone mean. Someone like Blackbeard."

Ming put her hands over her ears. "I don't hear you."

"Ming."

"I don't hear you," she repeated, without uncovering her ears. "You're just upset because I found her and you didn't."

"If Auntie Jove is real, why hasn't she written to *me* then, huh? I'm the oldest."

"Maybe she doesn't want to write to you. Maybe she wants to write to me, because she likes me best. You have Manny and I have Auntie Jove."

I remembered my father's face that day, at my mother's funeral. Vea saying *I didn't know Mei-Mei had a sister*. Was it that moment when I realized that Auntie Jove wasn't real? Or was it later, when Vea married my father in the same church where we had my mother's funeral? Was I still waiting for Auntie Jove when we crossed the ocean? It's easier to remember the first time you had a dream than the last. Dreams are like that. They're bright as stars at first, until they finally slip away and fade into the dark. But now Auntie Jove was back, only she wasn't my dream this time.

I looked hard at my little sister, standing there with her hands over her ears. I opened my arms wide, and let her fall into them.

❧ 11 ❧
The Curb

If you hang out long enough on Piedmont Avenue, you'll run into some kids from the Snout eventually. Since school was out and they weren't wearing uniforms, I couldn't be sure if they were Snout kids— especially since I found them skateboarding in an empty parking lot, which is the last place I expected to find them—but when I called out, "Hey, do you go to Strout?" as I walked up to them, the two guys and one girl stopped what they were doing and looked up.

"Yeah," the girl said. She was sitting on the curb, watching the boys do tricks on their skateboards. Except they weren't really doing any tricks, they were mostly tripping and sending their skateboards flying. They were dressed in beat-up T-shirts and jeans.

"Who're you?" the girl said. She had bleached blond hair with pink highlights. She shaded her eyes from the sun and stood up. The two boys went off down the lot on their skateboards. It was kind of cool, the sound the wheels made against the concrete. *Grrr-thmp, grrr-thmp, grrr-thmp.*

"I go to Leo," I said. "But I'm trying to find this girl who goes to your school."

"What's her name?"

"I don't know. That's the problem."

The girl tilted her head. "Why do you wanna find her?"

"I just gotta tell her something."

She paused and pressed her lips together the

same way I do when I'm thinking hard. "What's your name?"

"Soledad Madrid."

"What's she look like?"

"She's got real blond hair. Like, bright, bright blond. She walks kinda weird. She seems a little shy. I think she's . . . um . . . albino? Or something."

I could tell she knew who I was talking about.

"What do you need to tell her?" she asked. "Maybe I can pass it on."

I crossed my arms. "I'd rather tell her myself."

The girl looked toward the boys. They were too far away to hear us, but we could hear them. They pushed each other off their skateboards and swatted each other's arms. Then they made all kinds of crazy motions with their arms that made them look like monkeys.

Boys are so weird.

"I'm not gonna tell you who she is unless you tell me why you want to talk to her," the girl finally said.

"Why? What are you, her mother?"

She looked at me, square in the face, and said, "No. But some kids from Leo were messing with her yesterday and she had to get four stitches in her head. How do I know that wasn't *you*?"

My stomach did a nose dive.

I unfolded my arms and shoved my hands in the pockets of my cutoff shorts.

"It *was* me," I said. "That's what I wanna talk to her about."

"I heard there was a boy with you." She looked around the lot suspiciously. "Where's he?"

"He's not here. It's just me. I'm the one who hit her." I pulled my hair back and piled it on top of my head. I needed a rubber band. "Is she your friend?"

"No. But she's not my enemy."

"Fine. You don't have to tell me where she is. Just give her a message for me. Tell her I said that I'm sorry about the stitches. Okay?"

The girl didn't say anything, so I walked off. I

wanted to apologize to Casper in person, but I guess this was the best I could do.

I crossed the street and thought about those four stitches. They would probably leave a scar.

I wanted to cry—and I never cry.

I was almost too far away to hear the *grrr-thmp* of the skateboards when I heard the girl yell out, "Hey! Heeey!"

I turned around. She was standing right where I'd left her.

"Her name is Caroline Tilly!" She pointed down the block. "She lives at five twenty-one!"

That wanting-to-cry feeling didn't exactly disappear, but when I swallowed, it went away a little bit, like someone had loosened a tight knot in my stomach.

❧ 12 ❧

521 Piedmont Avenue

In the mysterious land north of Tippet's, there is a
house. It has two white columns out in front and
neat, straight bushes under big, bright windows.
There is a shiny black car in the driveway and a
shiny red one, too. There is a bicycle with a basket
in the yard and the yard is green, green, green. There
is a basketball hoop with a perfect white net, like it's
never been used. If you went around the world and
asked people what their idea of a Perfect American

Home would be, it would look something like this. It is 521 Piedmont Avenue, and there is something here that does not belong. It's a girl with messy black hair tied in a knot and cutoff jeans with a rip in the pocket. It's a girl with slanted eyes and a flat nose. It is me.

I dusted some of the dirt off my shorts, knocked on the door, and stood up as straight as possible, but then I realized that if I stood too straight, it looked like I was trying to stick out my chest, which looked stupid. So I just stood normally and stared at the blue paint on the door. I wondered what the house looked like inside. I wondered if it smelled like potpourri.

Vea got potpourri for our apartment last fall. She set it on the kitchen counter like it was something special. It looked really out of place, like a red rose in the middle of a patch of weeds. When I saw it, I took a big whiff until my head hurt, then asked, "What'd you get that for?"

"To make the place smell good," she said. "Why else?"

"Yeah, but you smoke like a chimney, so what's the point? You wanna have smoke that smells like roses?" I laughed. She smacked the back of my head and told me to go sit in the closet. When I told her I was too old for the closet, she spit in my hair and said I had two choices: sit in the closet or clean the whole apartment, from floor to ceiling. So I sat in the closet. While I was in there, I cleaned it. I pretended I had been trapped in a dungeon by a wicked dragon king. When I got out, I cleaned the bedroom for me and Ming. I spent hours just on that one room. I scrubbed until the carpet looked brand-new. Apartment four had never had such a clean room. I cleaned every inch. I scrubbed the doorframe with a toothbrush. It smelled like polish and money in that room when I was done. When Vea saw it, she said, "When you gonna do the rest of the house?" And she flicked her ashes on the clean carpet.

"I'm not," I said. "I picked the closet—remember?" Then I shut the door in her face.

I've shut doors in Vea's face plenty of times, but I've never really had one shut in mine. I kinda expected it would happen for the first time here on Piedmont Avenue, but instead a little girl with a curly blond ponytail opened the door and stood there.

"Hi," I said.

"Hi. I'm Constance. Are you here to see Christine?"

The scent of the house drifted out, and it smelled just like I thought it would: polish and potpourri. The cool air-conditioning felt so good that I wanted to dash inside and throw myself on the carpet.

"Um, no," I said. Constance. Christine. Caroline. Living on Piedmont Avenue was more complicated than I thought. "I'm here for Caroline."

"Really?"

"Yeah."

Constance shrugged, turned around, and hollered at the top of her lungs, "Caroline! Someone's at the door for you!" Then she took off and left me standing in the open doorway. A few seconds passed and I wondered if I'd been forgotten; maybe Caroline hadn't heard her and I'd just be left there, standing. I peeked into the living room and saw a big flat-screen television hanging over a fireplace, between two tall bookshelves. A bright rug on the floor. A heavy coffee table with a fancy candle on top. Matching living room set that looked like no one ever sat in it. I wondered what it was like to live in this house. I tried to imagine Vea living in a place like this, flicking her ashes on the floor.

I was just about to turn around and leave when someone breezed into the foyer—a tall girl with long blond hair and big blue eyes who looked like she'd just stepped out of a sunscreen commercial. When she saw me, she stopped and asked what I was doing.

"I'm waiting for Caroline," I explained.

Sunscreen Girl did the exact same thing that Constance did: she hollered, "CAROLINE!" Then she walked over to the couch, sat down, picked up the remote, and turned on the TV.

"You can come in, you know," she said. "You don't have to stand there." She sounded like she was very bored with every word she said.

Even though I really wanted to soak up that air-conditioning, I felt so weirdly out of place that I was going to say I'd rather wait outside, but then I heard the *thump-thump-thump* of someone coming down the stairs. It was Casper. She had a bandage above her right eyebrow—an eyebrow that was almost invisible since her hair was so blond. When she saw me, she frowned and touched her fingertips to it.

"Hey," she said.

"Hey."

The front door was still open. We walked outside and shut it behind us.

"Um," I said, looking away. I focused my eyes on the tops of the trimmed bushes. "My name is Sol Madrid. I'm the one who—" I pointed to my own eye and suddenly felt like a tremendous idiot—I was introducing myself, as if she wouldn't recognize me. "I just wanted to come by and . . ." I bit my bottom lip and looked at her. She was even more unusual looking now that we were standing so close. Her eyes were a pale shade of gray, surrounded by faint lines of red.

"And what?" she asked. Her voice was very quiet.

"Um . . ." I cleared my throat. "I wanted to say I was sorry. I'm really sorry about throwing that pinecone. It was stupid."

"Why did you throw it at me, anyway?"

"I don't know," I said. "Just goofing around, I guess."

She touched her bandage.

Just goofing around.

I was an idiot.

"Anyway," I said. "That's all. I'll go."

"Thanks for the apology," she said, quickly. Then she did something that I didn't expect: she smiled. Not a big, happy smile, but a smile nonetheless.

"Oh." I wasn't sure what to say. It didn't seem

right to be thanked for apologizing. So I just said, "You're welcome?" Like I was asking her a question.

"So does that mean you and your friend aren't going to throw things at me anymore?"

"Well . . ." I shrugged. "Yesterday was the last day of school, so . . ." I smiled back. "I guess not."

She laughed. It was a quiet laugh, but at least it was real. There's nothing worse than a fake laugh.

"That's true," she said.

I squinted up at the sun.

"Hey," I said. "Do you wanna get some bomb pops at Tippet's?"

She seemed surprised, like I'd asked her if she wanted to go backstage at a rock concert or something.

"Sure!" she said. "Let's go."

She headed quickly for the sidewalk, so I followed.

"Do you need to tell anyone you're leaving?" I asked.

"No," she said. "They never notice when I'm gone."

❈ 13 ❈

For Show

We didn't get bomb pops. Caroline bought us two giant sodas instead. It was a really balmy afternoon—the kind that makes you thirsty all day.

"Was that your sister?" I asked. We were sitting outside Tippet's on the milk crates.

"Yeah, both of them. The younger one is Constance. She's six." She shook the ice around in her soda. "Do you have any brothers or sisters?"

"Just sisters," I said. "Ming is six, too."

"How old are the other ones?"

I took a sip of my soda. "What other ones?"

"Your other sisters. You said you had more than one."

"Oh, I did?" Great. I never talked about Amelia. Only Manny knew I had a sister who died—and I didn't tell him the whole story, either. "Well, I used to have two sisters. But the other one died."

Caroline frowned. "That's terrible. Was she older or younger?"

"She was two years younger." I stared at a scorched patch of grass. "She died when she was five."

"How did she die?"

The cold cup numbed the palm of my hand.

"Do you always ask so many questions?" I said.

"Yep."

I banged the milk crate with my heel. "She drowned."

I could've just moved on to the next topic, like I

usually do. But for some reason I kept talking.

"One day we were walking to the market—me, my mom, and my sisters. I took off running. Just playing around, I guess. Somehow . . ."

Somehow the water swallowed Amelia. But I wasn't just playing around. I wanted my mother's attention. She kept fussing over Amelia and Ming, and I wanted to play. So I ran off, hid behind a coconut tree. Just for fun. My mother yelled at me to come out, but I didn't, so she turned away from my sisters to look for me. She didn't turn away long. She was a good mother. I should've come out the first time, but I'm stubborn. I'm selfish. I'm a terrible sister. I didn't come out until I heard my mother scream—but not at me. It was Amelia.

We sat in silence until Caroline said, "My other sister is sixteen. Her name's Christine. Constance, the younger one, is a cellist."

"Really? What's that mean?"

"She plays the cello in concerts."

"Like recitals?" I went to a piano recital once

for Manny's little sister. It was a few years ago and Manny begged me to go so he wouldn't be bored. It didn't work. We were both bored.

"More than a recital," said Caroline. "*Concerts*. People buy tickets. People from Juilliard, even. There was an article about her in the newspaper once."

I couldn't imagine paying money to sit through a recital, concert, or whatever it was, and I had no idea what Juilliard was. It sounded really impressive, though.

"What's your other sister do?" I asked. "She looks like a model."

Caroline shrugged. "Dates boys. Wins pageants." She pushed her straw in and out of the cup, making a scratchy sound. "She wants to be a model. But when she gets older, her looks will go away. Constance will be able to play the cello until she's old."

"Do you play any instruments?"

"No. My parents tried to teach me the piano, but I wasn't any good. I don't go to pageants, either. But I guess you figured that."

I hoped I wasn't frowning on the outside, because I felt like I was frowning on the inside.

"I'm really sorry about the stitches," I said. "I hope it doesn't leave a scar."

She touched her bandage. "I don't mind if it does."

"Really? Why?"

She shrugged. "It'll give me a story to tell. Well, not much of a story, anyway, but at least it's something interesting."

"Maybe you could *invent* a really good story," I said.

"Like what?"

"You could say that a boy was about to kiss you and you accidentally slammed heads."

"No one would believe that."

"Why not? Sometimes people accidentally bump heads when they're about to kiss." I didn't know if that was true or not, but it seemed possible.

"No one would ever believe that a boy would kiss

me." She sipped her soda. "What else you got?"

"Well . . . you could say that you saw a fairy in the woods behind your school and it hit you with a magic branch when you tried to catch it."

She laughed. "You have a good imagination."

"I get it from my mom. She died when I was eight, but I can still remember all the stories she told me."

Her smile faded. I wondered what she was thinking. Probably that I was cursed.

"Who do you live with now?" she asked.

"My stepmother. Vea."

"Is she nice?"

I cleared my throat. I thought about the potpourri and how she spit in my hair. I thought about the cold water on my skin. And I thought about 521 Piedmont Avenue and how it looked and smelled. I didn't want to tell Caroline another sad story. So I said, "Oh, yeah. She's great. We're really close, the three of us—me, my sister, and Vea. My dad died, too, a couple years ago, so we're, like, orphans. But Vea takes care of us. One time she even took us to the French Quarter just so we could get our fortunes read."

"Seriously?" said Caroline. "What was it like?"

"This old, hunchbacked lady told me and my sister that we would live long lives, and she told me that one day I would create something magnificent. That's the word she used—*magnificent*. And she told me that my mother was proud of me and that she was safe."

"Wow." Caroline's eyes were round. "She could communicate with your mom?"

"Oh, yeah. All those fortune-tellers can. The ones that are real, anyway. There's a lot of scammers out there, but not her. She knew things that she wouldn't have been able to know unless she was really psychic. Like, she described our house and everything. It was *so* weird."

"I bet," said Caroline. "I've always believed in that stuff, but if you told that to my dad, he would say that anyone could describe a house and make it sound like your house."

I shook my head. "This lady gave details. And it

was hard, too, because our house is pretty big. Not as big as your house, but it's still pretty big. We have a fireplace, too, like you."

She rolled her eyes. "We don't even use our fireplace. My mom says there's no point because it never really gets cold. So I asked her why we got a fireplace if we weren't gonna use it. And she says it's for show." She pulled up her straw and pushed it down again and again. "She likes things that are just for show."

We sat there for a little while, feeling the sun.

"Did the stitches hurt?" I asked.

"Yeah, kinda." She touched them again. It seemed like a habit. I could see why she would keep touching them, though. "It hurt a lot worse than the pinecone, if that makes you feel any better. If I wouldn't have had to get stitches, the pinecone wouldn't have been a big deal."

Here she was, trying to make me feel better about giving her stitches. Even worse, she didn't seem to mind having them because it gave her something interesting to say.

I cleared my throat and looked down at my hands. "Caroline?"

"Yeah?"

"I lied."

"Lied? About what?"

"I don't have a big house."

When I looked up at her, she smiled.

"It's okay," she said. "Big houses aren't as exciting as they seem. I have a big house and all I do is daydream about getting out of it and going somewhere interesting."

"And my stepmom. Vea . . ."

"Did you make her up, too?"

"I wish." I shook my soda and listened to the ice cubes shuffle against each other. "The other day she poured cold water on me and pinched my nose so hard that I thought it would break. Sometimes she spits in my hair."

Caroline frowned.

I didn't say anything.

After a few silent moments had passed, Caroline said, "Yesterday my mother didn't speak to me at all."

What gloomy tales we had, I thought. I wondered what we'd look like to someone passing by. Two twelve-year-old girls—one so white she looked like a ghost and the other so dark she looked like the fields—sitting on milk crates and telling sad, sad stories in the hot, hot sun.

✖ 14 ✖
Thieves

After Caroline went home, I decided to wander by Alcott Park, which is only a few blocks down from the Tower. Who knows? Maybe they had a tree house for Ming.

I hadn't been to Alcott Park in a long, long time because Vea said it was "ruled by thugs." You'd think a park would be a nice place, but Alcott has a bad reputation. Sometimes on the news you hear, "On the corner of Alcott and so-and-so today . . ." and the rest of the sentence is never anything good. But I figured maybe things had gotten better. You never know.

Unfortunately, I was wrong.

Not only did Alcott Park not have any tree houses, it didn't have any trees. And the playground equipment looked like something from the dark ages. There weren't any kids around, either. Just two teenagers in Saints hoodies smoking by the tire swings and that lady who'd been cursing at the mailboxes the other day. Her hair was in a bun, like usual, and she was wearing her casino uniform. She was sitting on one of the benches, talking really loudly on her cell phone. She was speaking another language— Chinese, I guess—but every other word was an English curse word.

Alcott Park was no place for Ming.

I started making my way home.

Maybe I could build Ming a tree house after all. If I had supplies or money, maybe I could. If not a tree house, a clubhouse. How hard could it be? Nailing a few boards together couldn't be the hardest thing in the world. Maybe Manny's dad could help out when he wasn't busy on his gardening jobs. Only, he tended to be kinda mean when he wasn't working. So that might not be a good idea. It would just have to be me and Manny.

But not today.

Today, all I wanted to do was lie in bed and read. But when I reached my street, I saw Ming up ahead and immediately knew something was wrong. She had her arms wrapped around her belly and she was walking very fast and looking over her shoulder. I squinted at her as she hurried closer.

"Ming?" I said.

Now I realized why she was clutching her belly. She had something hidden under her shirt. Because Ming was so small, the something looked gigantic.

"What are you hiding?" I said. I thought maybe it was a cat. I wasn't prepared for what she pulled out:

a stationery set with envelopes. I took it from her. It was decorated with clouds and birds. "Where did you get this?"

Ming pressed her lips together tight, like she was deciding whether to tell me or not.

"Tippet's," she said finally.

"Where'd you get the money?"

"I had some saved up. It wasn't that expensive."

I turned the package over. It was seven dollars.

"You had seven dollars randomly saved up?" I asked.

She nodded silently.

"Where's the receipt, then? Where's the bag?"

"Um." She looked behind her, as if they could be found there. "I threw them away."

I raised my eyebrows. "Ming. Tell me the truth."

"I am."

"Did you steal this?"

I could see her thinking. She shook her head.

"Honestly?" I asked.

"I need it to write letters to Auntie Jove. Besides, you and Manny take stuff from there all the time."

I didn't know she knew that.

"We take bomb pops every now and then. They only cost a dollar. This is, like, a real product."

"And bomb pops aren't real products?"

"You know what I mean."

"I need it to write letters."

"You can write letters on normal paper."

"No. I want fancy paper."

"Then you'll have to save up your money and buy it the right way."

"But I never have any money."

"Then I guess you don't get fancy paper." I took her hand. "Come on. We're going to return it."

"I don't want to! I'll get in trouble!"

"No, you won't. We'll just put it right back where you got it. We won't tell Imani or Maria or anyone. We'll just put it right on the shelf, like it never left."

"I don't want to, though!" She yanked her hand

back, but I pulled. She bent her knees, trying to stand her ground. Her sneakers skid against the concrete. "I want to write to Auntie Jove on this fancy paper! You and Manny steal all the time!"

"We don't steal all the time. Besides, we don't even do that anymore because we know how stupid it is."

To be honest, Manny and I never planned on stealing the bomb pops. I don't even remember how it started. But no matter what, I couldn't have Ming shoplifting seven-dollar stationery. Even if that meant no more ice cream for me.

My plan was to take Ming right back to the supply section so she could put the stationery back where she found it. I didn't expect that she had already been caught and Imani and Maria would be near the entrance of the store with their arms crossed, like two security guards who were expecting criminals at any moment.

Unfortunately, *we* were the criminals.

"Ming, Ming, Ming!" Maria said, wagging her finger just like a mother scolding her own child. Next to her, Imani shook her head. Her gold hoop earrings brushed against her cheeks.

"I was just debating whether or not to come after you, little girl," Imani said. She motioned toward the stationery. "Hand it over." She didn't look angry. Just disappointed.

I put my arm around Ming's shoulders as she handed the box to Imani.

"If you wanted some colored paper, I could've brought you some from home," Imani said, frowning. She glanced down at the box. "It may not have clouds on it, but it's blue."

"She wanted to use it to write letters," I said. "But that's no excuse. Right, Ming?"

Ming pressed her lips together.

"You should apologize," I said, quietly.

Ming took a deep breath and said, "Sorry." Not rudely, but quickly—like she was ripping off a Band-Aid.

"It's okay," said Imani.

"I've already called Miss Vea, just so you know," Maria added. "You might be in trouble when you get home, but it's only because I know you're a good little girl. You don't know how many kids we see in here, stealing this and that, without any parents to intervene. And they always wind up getting in more and more trouble. Good to have a mother looking out for you."

My heart stopped beating. I felt Ming tense and freeze under my arm.

Why did they call Vea? Why?

I swallowed. "She's not our mother."

Maria looked at me suspiciously.

"She's our *step*mother," I corrected.

Neither Imani nor Maria said anything at first.

"Either way, she wants what is best for you," said Maria, finally.

My anger was hot now. So hot that I snapped, "What makes you think that?" I knew that my tone was rude. Maria was an adult, and I was being "sharp-tongued," as my teachers liked to say. But she didn't know what she was talking about. If she did, she would have never called Vea. Never.

"Ming said . . ." Maria eyed my sister, clearly confused.

She didn't finish, but she didn't need to. I didn't know what Ming had told them about her life with Vea. Probably fairy tales. But it didn't matter. What was done was done.

Vea was waiting.

When we walked through the door, she was sitting on the couch, wearing her slippers, with the volume on the television turned all the way down. Mr. Elephant sat next to her, staring at the flat, voiceless faces on the TV screen with his black, beaded eyes.

I took a long swift step toward the couch to snatch him up, but Vea was expecting me. She grabbed him and stood.

Ming screamed. She kept screaming until she started coughing. She coughed and coughed and coughed, burst into loud sobs, and crumpled onto the floor like a deflated balloon.

"Mousy *kano!*" said Vea. "Stealing, like a thief! Like a mousy little thief! Making me look dirty and pathetic!"

"You don't need any help in that department," I said.

Vea narrowed her eyes. "No one is speaking to *you.*"

"*I'll* talk for Ming. She doesn't have to speak to you if she doesn't want to."

"Yes, you're right," said Vea. "Because you speak enough for the both of you. I can't get her to talk, and I can't make *you* shut up. If you don't learn when to shut that dirty trap of yours, you will live your life alone and the only kind of man you will have is a little coward. Someone like your father."

"Maybe she doesn't want to speak to you because

you're an evil witch," I said. I wasn't going to explode. I didn't want to give Vea the pleasure of making me angry.

Vea threw her head back and laughed. "If I were an evil witch, I would kick both of you American girls out onto the street. I have no need or use for you." She shoved Mr. Elephant under her armpit and lit a cigarette. "Your father left me with you, but I have no obligation. We are in America now, little girls." She blew smoke in my face, but I didn't cough or flinch, even though the smell was the most disgusting thing in the whole world. "That mouse will speak to me and explain how she became a dirty thief. I will *make* her speak, if I have to."

She took one more puff on her cigarette and then put it out on Mr. Elephant's head. Ming didn't see, though. She was whimpering and curled on the floor with her eyes closed.

I reached for Mr. Elephant, but Vea dodged me and pushed her cigarette deeper and deeper into his head. It smelled like burning paper. Mr. Elephant was too soft to put the smoke out right away, so Vea dropped the cigarette on the carpet and stamped it with her foot.

"You're an evil witch!" I said.

"This dirty toy!" Vea hollered. She held Mr. Elephant in front of her like he was a soiled sock, but every time I tried to grab him, she yanked him away. "Why do you want a toy that is made of lies, eh, *kano*? Your father doesn't love you, you little mouse! Did you know that? He doesn't love you. He told me so."

My insides shook like a volcano ready to burst into flames and burn everything around me. My eyes filled with tears, but they were angry tears, the kind that you don't want to have, but they come anyway, shaky and unstoppable.

"THAT'S A LIE! MY FATHER WOULD NEVER SAY THAT ABOUT ME OR MING! YOU'RE A LIAR!"

"Your father didn't have to tell me; I *knew*! What kind of father leaves his children behind? And for what? For some other woman! A woman, *kano*!" She grabbed Mr. Elephant with both hands now and tried to rip him apart in midair. The threads pulled and pulled. They clung like teeth, desperate to keep him together.

"You're evil!" I yelled. My face felt hot and sticky. "You're the devil!"

Vea stopped pulling at Mr. Elephant and glared at me. I waited for her to do something terrible—to punch me in the nose or kick me to the ground. I vowed right then and there to smash every last one of her stupid plants, and I would have, but before anything more could happen there were four loud knocks on the door. *Knock, knock, knock, knock.*

Ming got quiet.

Vea shot me a hard glare, shoved Mr. Elephant under her disgusting arm, and threw open the door. Mrs. Yeung was standing there in her pajamas.

"What?" asked Vea, irritated. "What, old woman?"

Mrs. Yeung leaned her head to the side and

peered into our little apartment. The sight of her there, looking like a bronze statue, scared me.

"What do you want?" Vea asked Mrs. Yeung.

Mrs. Yeung looked at Ming. Then at me.

Please give us some money from your safe, Mrs. Yeung, I thought. *Then me and Ming could run away and go someplace better. Anyplace.*

For a moment I thought she understood me, because something sparked in her eyes. But then she simply turned and left. Vea shut the door behind her.

"No use coming to this country if you can't even speak English," said Vea. She kissed the top of Mr. Elephant's head, right where she'd burned him, and walked slowly toward Ming. "You can have him back, *kano,* when you decide to behave like an obedient girl." When Ming didn't look up or respond, Vea kicked her foot.

"You're a stupid mouse, like your mother," said Vea.

I didn't move. I couldn't. I felt like if I moved, something terrible would happen.

Maybe I would cry and never stop.

Maybe I would scream until all the windows shattered.

Maybe I would just break apart like glass.

"It doesn't matter," said Ming. "Auntie Jove is coming soon. I wasn't going to tell you, because I knew you wouldn't believe me, but it's true. Auntie Jove is coming on June third."

Ming was sitting in the corner of the closet and I was at the foot of the bed.

I sighed. "Ming . . ."

"I don't care if you don't believe me."

"Ming . . ."

She brought her knees to her chest and rested her chin on top of them. "I don't care if no one ever believes me. It won't matter anyway. When Auntie Jove comes, you'll see."

I opened my mouth to argue, but closed it again and nodded slowly.

We sat in silence for a while, staring at different parts of the room.

Finally I said, "We can find Mr. Elephant. We'll just have to wait for the right time to search Vea's room."

"All we have to do is wait," said Ming. "Wait until June third."

"What she said about Papa isn't true, Ming."

Ming looked away. "I didn't hear anything she said."

"I know you heard."

She closed her eyes. "I didn't hear anything."

"It isn't true, the things she said. He isn't a good papa, but that doesn't mean that he doesn't love us." Even as I said it, I wasn't sure I believed it. After all, Vea was right. What kind of father leaves his children alone in another country with someone like Vea and then never comes back? Never even calls?

"Some papas love their children. They just don't do a good job taking care of them. It's not because of us. It has nothing to do with us."

She turned so she was facing away from me, toward the back of the closet. "I don't even know what you're talking about," she said, quietly. "I didn't hear anything, like I said."

But I knew she did. When someone says something like that, you can't help but hear. I would've heard Vea even if I was five miles away.

"Good," I said. "Because it was all lies, anyway."

"It doesn't matter. All we have to do is wait. Wait until June third. Then I'll get Mr. Elephant back and we'll be rescued, just like princesses." She paused. "Maybe I'll stay in here until June third. I'll fix it up and it'll be even better than the tree house at school. It doesn't matter that there's no ladder. If Vea comes, all I have to do is shut the door."

What could I say? That princesses don't really get rescued? That our closet would always be a closet? That two kids with no money can't really go anywhere on June third or any other day? That she would never have a tree house or anything else, really?

"You could say the truth."

It was Amelia, in the corner.

I took a deep breath. "Which part?" I whispered. "The part where no one is going to rescue us or the part where she'll never have anything?"

"The part where the closet is a closet, but it's also a rocket or a tree house. The part where your mind is a palace, as long as you go in the right rooms."

Sometimes Amelia talked in riddles. Sometimes she talked like our mother.

"How do you know what the right rooms are?" I asked.

Amelia thought about this. The whites of her eyes glistened. Her mouth turned upward. A smile.

"You ask your sister," she said.

❈ 15 ❈
Dragon

There's no way my mother was perfect, but that's how I remember her. The only person who would say any different is Vea, and I don't trust anything she says.

"Your father would never have come to America if not for me," Vea said one afternoon, soon after he left us. "She would have held him back for the rest of his life."

I was doing my homework on the living room

floor at the time. I didn't look at her when she spoke. Instead, I slammed my hand on top of my paper and ripped it out of my notebook in one big movement. Then I balled it up and looked directly at my evil stepmother. She glared down at me from the raggedy sofa.

My chest swelled. That's what it felt like, at least. It swelled up like a water balloon, ready to pop. But I wouldn't cry in front of Vea. Never. Instead, I decided to shove the crumpled paper in her mouth. But when I tried to, my arm was as heavy as a brick. Like I was too angry to move. And Vea just kept glaring at me. Daring me to do something. That's what she wanted—she wanted me to shove the paper in her mouth or yell out and defend my mother. That way she could be meaner. Hurt me more. But I wouldn't let her.

I uncrumpled the paper. Smoothed it out calmly with the palms of my hands.

"A lot of good it did my father," I said. "He went

right back to the Philippines. So maybe he would never have come if not for you, but he went back. And you're still here."

Vea's face hardened. "That's true, *kano*," she said. "But so are you."

When I was younger, I invented a story about Vea. I imagined that she'd been born from the mouth of a three-headed dragon. The second head spit her out in a spray of fire and she landed, fully grown, on a bed of spindly pine needles, wearing that red lipstick that bewitched my father. Seven seconds after she was born, she shook the cinders from her hair and it turned black as coal.

Being born from a dragon sucks out a lot of your oxygen, so her cheeks were sunken in and her body was thin like a knobby stick.

That was the story I repeated to myself the night my father told me he was marrying Vea and she was coming with us to America. At the time he was trying to mend the strap of one of my sandals with a needle and thread. He'd poked himself three times already—further evidence, he said, that he needed a woman around.

"But she's mean," I said.

"No. She's stern. And that's what you and Ming need. A stern mother to watch after you."

"Can't we stay with someone else?"

"There is no one else."

"Can't we . . ." *find Auntie Jove?*

"Can't we what, Soledad?"

"Never mind."

So the Dragon Queen inherited two little girls she didn't want, and who didn't want her, either, all so she could get a husband and come to America. Eventually her red lips faded and she settled down on her perch on the secondhand sofa of an infested dungeon. The only signs of her previous life were the wisps of smoke drifting from her nose and mouth.

✕ 16 ✕
Ready

Things I know to be true: When Manny pulls his baseball cap over his eyes and claps his hands once, this means trouble, like he wants to prank people and knock on doors and take off running or decorate street signs with Magic Marker.

"Whatcha wanna do today, huh?" He flicked the back of my ear lightly as we stepped out of the lobby of the Tower. The air was wet and the sky was gray. Rain was coming. "Whatcha wanna do? Huh? Huh?"

Sometimes Manny sounds like a clucking chicken.

"Junkyard," I said, swatting his hand away. I hate when he flicks my ear but when I tell him to stop, he doesn't—he just flicks it more.

When we stepped down from the stoop, I saw Mrs. Yeung standing on the curb with her hands on her hips. She was staring across the street, even though there was nothing there but an empty field overgrown with yellowed grass and old tires.

Manny and I exchanged looks. He circled his index finger around his ear. *Crazy.* But I thought of those four knocks. *Knock, knock, knock, knock. Don't worry, girls. Someone's listening. Someone's watching.*

I hadn't told Manny about that.

Mrs. Yeung didn't turn when we passed by.

Once we were out of earshot, Manny said, "What do you think she's doing when she stares into space like that? And why are we going to the freakin' junkyard?"

He doesn't like the junkyard. He thinks I don't

know that, but I do. And I know exactly why he doesn't like it, even though he would never admit it. It's not because of Blackbeard. It's because of his dog. The Beast.

"I have a project I wanna work on and I need to have it done by June third," I explained as we walked.

"Project? What kind of project?"

"You'll see."

"You're not doing . . . schoolwork, are you?" He clutched his T-shirt and pretended to have a heart attack.

"No. I want to build Ming a tree house."

"You're kidding, right?"

"No. I'm not kidding."

"And what tree are you gonna put it in? That one?" He pointed at a skimpy tree across the street that looked half dead.

"I don't know. I haven't thought that far."

"I'm pretty sure you can't just put a tree house

anywhere you want. Plus, we don't know how to build anything," said Manny. "And Blackbeard isn't gonna have a random tree house hanging around for us to pick up. And how would we get a tree house over the fence anyway? Or any of the supplies? We should get, like, summer jobs or something instead. Then we can just buy whatever supplies you need to—"

"Do you ever shut up?"

He took two quick steps and wrapped his arm around my waist. "Kiss me and I'll shut up."

I pushed him off. He stumbled into the patch of dead grass in front of the free clinic, a square brick building that was always giving away free flu shots, health screenings, stuff like that. There was a big sign out front that said "FREE CLINIC" in capital letters, right next to a picture of a dove carrying a leaf in its mouth. Vea took me there when I had the stomach flu and she said the dove was a symbol of peace, but she didn't know what was so peaceful about sitting in a room like packed rats. Then she went up to the ladies at the front desk and yelled that there would be trouble if I threw up on her shoes because the doctor was taking his sweet time.

"You're just scared of the Beast," I said. "That's why you don't wanna go."

When you live south of Tippet's you have to worry about people stealing your stuff. One way to stop people from swiping your lawn mower or car speakers is to have an enormous hungry dog with sharp teeth standing in front of everything you own.

Blackbeard probably knows that his junkyard is an easy target. It's in the middle of a big, open field of half-dead grass. The people in the Tower aren't too bad, but there are plenty of other apartment buildings around and some of them are a little dicey. They all have stupid names, too. Paradise Manor, Pecan Grove, Crescent Estates. You'd think we were living in a fairy tale, not in a place where you have to worry about your car speakers getting stolen.

At the edge of all these manors and estates is Blackbeard's junkyard. It's set back from the road and surrounded by a chain-link fence, but the fence is easy to climb. There's a camper in the center of it. That's where Blackbeard lives. He's short and burly, with a thick, thick beard that he grows all year, even in the summer. He wears dirty overalls and carries that pellet gun, just in case.

The Beast lives outside, on a chain. I'm not sure what he's chained to. Maybe the camper.

You know you're getting close to the junkyard when you reach the biggest crack in the sidewalk—the one that looks like the earth has erupted in that one spot. It was like a crooked cement pyramid.

"If that dog even looks at me sideways . . ." said Manny, but he didn't finish because we stepped over the pyramid crack, and the open field and the fence came into view.

"Ready?" I said.

I didn't wait for him to answer. I ran for the fence.

❧ 17 ❧
Land of What

The Beast always knows when you're coming. I read somewhere that a dog's sense of smell is ten thousand times stronger than a human's. So you can't pull a fast one on the Beast. To be honest, I'd be afraid of him too if he wasn't chained up. Plus the chain is thick and heavy, just like his collar.

I landed on the other side of the fence on both feet and crouched down so Blackbeard wouldn't see me. I heard Manny land behind me, but I didn't move. You have to keep your eye on the ball in these types of situations.

I peered between tilted stacks of hubcaps, rearview mirrors, and wheel rims. Blackbeard had the junkyard arranged like a city with neighborhoods—car parts over here, pipes and mechanical-looking stuff over there, mounds and mounds of old glass bottles just around the corner. There was also a spot for random things, like street signs and old restaurant booths. In any direction you could find discarded tin sheds, doors, corroded metal, rusty bicycles missing their wheels, wheels missing their bicycles, dead power tools, dead mowers, white refrigerators that had turned brown, and hills made up of all kinds of other stuff. The whole junkyard smelled like oil. In the center of it all was Blackbeard's small white camper.

I saw the Beast from my vantage point, and I know he saw me—or smelled me, at least. He lifted his square head and perked up his pointed ears. He was a big, black dog. There was a circle of skin on his back where he didn't have any fur. The chain dangled from his thick neck. He was lying on a round patch of dirt.

Manny inched up next to me.

"Do you think—"

"Shh," I said, waving my hand in front of his face to shut him up. "Wait."

We waited until the Beast put his head back down. Then I stood up and motioned for Manny to follow me. We stepped lightly. It's not easy to be quiet in a junkyard.

"So, what are we looking for?" he hissed as we maneuvered around yet another pile of hubcaps. "What are we doing here?"

"I told you, I want to build Ming a tree house. Help me look for stuff." I thought about the day my mother lined up the chairs and we pretended to sail for America. "Maybe it doesn't have to be a tree house. A canoe, maybe. Or a rowboat."

"A *rowboat*? Are you crazy? How are we supposed to get a boat out of here?"

"Look for anything good. Maybe we can toss it over the fence and do something with it later."

Manny shook his head but didn't argue. He walked a few feet away and started sorting through some junk. I did the same thing. We did that for a good while, shifting from one pile to another and glancing over our shoulders now and then to make sure Blackbeard and his Beast weren't coming after us. It was easy to believe that there was a giant oven inside that camper, just big enough to fit two or more kids inside.

Within an hour we were both drenched with sweat, smelled like grease and oil, and had a few nicks and scratches from picking up old metal and other scraps. Manny did his best to find interesting things, but every time he held something up to show me—a stick shift, a cracked mirror, a broken parking meter—I shook my head.

By the time we reached the big bin of license plates, I was thirsty and daydreaming about getting ice cream at Tippet's, but I insisted that we sort through the plates anyway.

"We need to leave with something," I said.

"I still don't even know what we're looking for," Manny mumbled. "And I haven't seen any *rowboats*. Plus, I . . ."

He kept talking, but I tuned him out. I'd discovered a beat-up license plate that looked kind of good. It's hard to explain why some things look interesting. I held it up and studied it. It was from Illinois. It said "Go Cubs." Across the bottom, in small letters, it said "Land of." There was more, but I couldn't make out the rest. All I could see was an N.

"You rejected the parking meter, but you pick up something like that?" said Manny. He took off his hat and shook the sweat out of his hair. The brim of his cap was smudged with grease.

"'Land of,'" I read. "Land of what?"

The Beast barked.

Manny and I flinched and a stack of rearview mirrors clattered beside us. That got the Beast barking even more. The problem was, we couldn't see him. We were surrounded by hubcaps.

"Crap!" cried Manny. He stumbled back, his eyes darting in every direction.

We couldn't tell if the barks were nearby or faraway. Just that they were angry and loud. The kind of barks that said, *Dinner's here, Blackbeard! Come and get it!*

Manny turned and made a fast sprint toward the fence. I saw him slip. Scramble back up. Take down a mound of headlights.

"Don't run or it'll chase you!" I yelled. My heart thumped. My whole body felt like it was on fire. The Beast would come bounding out of the junk, slobbering and drooling and hungry for flesh. I just knew it. The Beast would chase after Manny, or soar over the hubcaps and bury its claws in my eyes. Maybe rip my ears with its teeth.

Should I stand there frozen or make for the fence at a slow, steady pace?

Or should I just run for it?

I decided to run for it.

I was still holding the license plate.

✖ 18 ✖

Apartment Three

Even though the Tower was the only place in America I had ever lived, I'd never knocked on a single door there other than my own, and that was only when Vea locked me out. After saying good-bye to Manny and hiding my Illinois plate in the closet, I tied my now-greasy hair into a ponytail, cleaned up some of the scrapes on my arms, and went to visit Mrs. Yeung. Manny was right—maybe we could get summer jobs to earn some money. Only, who would hire a twelve-year-old? An old, lonely lady with thousands of dollars, that's who.

It took several knocks before she opened the door, but I knew she was home because I heard the clinking and clanking of dishes. When she finally opened the door, she didn't say a word. She was wearing a long housedress and her gray hair was pulled back in a bandanna.

"Hi, Mrs. Yeung," I said, tacking on my best smile. "I was wondering if you have anything you need done this summer. I'm trying to earn some extra money."

She didn't answer. Instead, she stepped aside and opened the door even wider.

The layout of Mrs. Yeung's apartment was exactly like ours, but the spaces couldn't have been more different. We didn't have much in our apartment, but Mrs. Yeung had plenty, mostly books and bookcases. There were books stacked on the television, under the coffee table, in the corners, and on top of just about every flat surface. There were even a few books in the kitchen.

The apartment smelled faintly like rice, but also had another smell: pages, hardcovers and paperbacks, like the library at school. I felt like I'd entered another universe.

"Did you need me to help with the cleaning?" I asked, looking around. I hoped she had an easier task for me.

Mrs. Yeung didn't answer. She put her hand under my elbow and guided me toward her old couch, where I sat down. Then she went into the kitchen and clanked around some more.

"I can do those dishes for you, Mrs. Yeung," I called. "I won't even charge that much."

I looked at the books stacked up on the coffee table in front of me. The titles were all in another language. Chinese? I wondered what they were about.

"Maybe I should just go back home," I said. "I didn't mean to interrupt you if you were busy—"

I stood up just as she came back holding a tray with a teapot and two cups. I pushed aside some of the books so she could set it down.

"Oh," I said. "Thank you. I've never actually had tea before."

She sat next to me on the couch and filled two cups. The tea looked like light-brown water and there were a few flaky leaves floating around. I didn't really want to drink it, but I didn't want to be rude, either, so I picked up the cup the same way she did.

"I'm not sure if you speak any English or not," I said, taking a tiny sip. It didn't taste as bad as I thought it would. "If not, maybe I can give you some lessons. I won't charge that much. English is my second language, too. I learned it from the time I was a little girl in the Philippines, but my native dialect is Cebuano. I've forgotten most of it, though. My little sister, Ming, doesn't remember any of it. My stepmother does, but I don't like talking to her, so . . ."

I took another sip. Mrs. Yeung did, too. "Actually, Ming is part of the reason I'm here. I'm working on this project for her. It may sound silly, but I want to build her something." I put the teacup down and looked hard at Mrs. Yeung, hoping there was something in her face that showed me she understood. "Do you have any brothers or sisters?" I asked. When she didn't answer, I said, "Ming is really the only family I have. My father left us. He left us with my stepmother. I guess you probably know that." I looked down at my tea. I watched the leaves float around near the bottom of the cup. "We call her our evil stepmother. Like in the fairy tales? My real mother, she used to tell us fairy tales, but she'd make up her own. Sometimes she would load us in this imaginary sailboat and take us all over the world, but it was just in our heads. I bet she never thought we'd end up here in America without her." I swallowed.

What was wrong with me? I couldn't stop talking.

"I wonder what she would think of us being stuck here with Vea. My mother is nothing like Vea. Vea is—"

And then the strangest thing happened: When

I said Vea's name, I heard her voice. Not in the apartment, but in a muffled, faraway place, like she was hiding in one of Mrs. Yeung's cabinets. My head popped up. I looked at Mrs. Yeung to see if she'd heard it, too, but she was drinking her tea. I wondered if she was deaf.

I could only make out a few words. There was a creaking sound, too, like she was pacing. That's when I realized it was coming from one of Mrs. Yeung's air vents. Vea was on the phone and her voice was traveling through the vents and into Mrs. Yeung's living room. It wasn't loud and clear, but it was irritating nonetheless.

"I don't know if you can hear that," I said, my eyes traveling to the corners of the room as I listened, "but that's Vea. She really *is* an evil stepmother. She stole my sister's stuffed giraffe. It's a giraffe, but Ming calls him Mr. Elephant." My voice caught in my throat at the thought of Mr. Elephant. I looked into Mrs. Yeung's eyes again, even though she wasn't really looking at me and still hadn't said a word. "Anyway, it's because of Ming that I need some odd jobs. I want to build her a tree house, or something, but I don't have any supplies."

Mrs. Yeung finished her tea and put her cup down. I'd spent the past ten minutes talking to an old woman who either didn't understand English, couldn't hear, or both. But I didn't care. I felt better talking to someone, even if she couldn't help me.

I stood up. "Thanks for your time, Mrs. Yeung. Let me know if you ever need someone to do odd jobs. I'm in apartment four, right next door."

She stood up, too. She took my arm again and held up her index finger. *Wait.* This time she walked down the hall and left me standing there in her living room with my hands shoved in my back pockets.

When she came back, she was holding a black bag in one hand and a small bottle in the other. She motioned for me to sit on the couch, so I did. I suspected that the bag was full of rocks, marbles, or maybe coins, so when she emptied it out on the coffee table, I was surprised. It was full of bracelets and rings. Lots of them. Maybe twenty or thirty pieces of jewelry altogether. They looked really old.

Mrs. Yeung sat next to me and picked through the pile with her finger, which was skinny and wrinkled and reminded me of old paper. Every now and then she held up a piece of jewelry to show off—a ring with a pale yellow gem, a bracelet of faded gold, a chipped bangle. I stared at one in particular for a long time, a bracelet of black pearls. The pearls weren't perfect and shiny like the ones you usually see. They were flawed and misshapen, like they'd just been plucked out of an oyster's mouth.

"Wow," I said.

For a crazy moment I thought she was giving me all this jewelry. I imagined how excited Ming would be to get a mysterious bag of jewels. But then Mrs. Yeung unscrewed the bottle, emptied a small amount onto a tiny rag that had fallen out with the rings and bracelets, and polished one of the bangles carefully until it shined. Then she nudged the rag into my hands.

"Oh, you want me to clean these?" I said. "Okay, I can do that. Let's say, ten dollars to polish the whole set?" I raised my eyebrows, but Mrs. Yeung wasn't paying any attention. She was heading back to the kitchen. I sighed and started polishing.

It took me a while to finish, but it was easy work and I barely had a thought in my head the whole time. I got lost in each piece. The tiny gold ring had belonged to a miniature duchess who lived in a dollhouse. The thick silver necklace once adorned Magellan's neck as he sailed around the world. The ruby earrings with clip-on clasps? Those had been the beloved treasure of a kidnapped Chinese empress.

When I was done, my hands smelled like lemons.

Mrs. Yeung had disappeared into one of the bedrooms after she finished the dishes. I figured she was taking a nap or something. I stood up and politely called out her name. A few seconds later she appeared.

So she's not deaf after all.

I smiled and motioned to the jewelry. "I finished them. They look great."

She examined my work. Her eyes were kind and gray. I watched them move over each piece. The folds of her skin looked soft and tired. It was hard to imagine she was twelve once.

I shoved my hands into my back pockets again. After rummaging through the junkyard and polishing all this stuff, I was ready to get home and take a hot shower.

"Ten dollars?" I asked. "If that's too much, maybe seven."

Mrs. Yeung hooked her papery finger around the pearl bracelet and held it out to me.

"Are you giving this to me?" I said, stupidly. It was obvious that's exactly what she was doing. When she laid it in my palm, I wasn't sure if I was happy or disappointed. No ten dollars. Instead, a bracelet that could be worth a penny for all I knew. "Oh," I said. "Thank you, Mrs. Yeung." I wrapped the bracelet around my wrist and clasped it. It was a little big, but not too big to wear. It looked kinda nice, actually, even though it didn't really match my dirty summer clothes.

I stepped into the hallway and thanked her again.

Mrs. Yeung nodded—did that mean *you're welcome*?—before she gently closed the door.

❈ 19 ❈
Suitcase

It was raining on the day we left for America. The Philippines has many rainy days. Even on the days when it isn't raining, it feels like it could at any minute. The sun may be high and bright, but there's a feeling of dampness all around. Sometimes it smells like wet grass.

Ming was really little then, but she had her own suitcase that our papa bought for her. It was almost as big as she was. It was decorated with bright, tropical flowers. Like many traveling Filipinos we had packed most of our things in our *balikbayan* box, but Papa wanted Ming to have a suitcase of her own. That was the only time she ever used it. After we moved into the Tower, I slipped it under the bed. When I came back from Mrs. Yeung's, there it was, open on the floor of our room.

It's strange when you see something from your past like that—something that triggers all kinds of memories. When I saw that suitcase, I remembered how the air felt in Cebu on the day we left and how it felt when we landed in New Orleans. I remembered the strained look on our father's face on the long, long plane ride over the ocean, and how Vea purred in his ear with her bright red lips. I remembered Ming falling asleep on my shoulder.

"What're you doing?" I asked. I closed the door so Vea wouldn't hear us, even though she was asleep in her bedroom and she never heard anything when she was sleeping.

Ming was sitting cross-legged on the floor next to

a pile of her clothes. She was holding her locked box of letters from Auntie Jove.

"Packing," she said, like I'd asked a stupid question. "June third is coming soon and I don't want to waste even a single minute. I'm not packing everything, though. I put some clothes aside to wear between now and when she comes. I'm also trying to figure out if there are any clothes that don't fit me anymore. We can give them to Auntie Jove and she'll donate them to kids in need."

I crossed my arms. "*We're* kids in need."

"You know what I mean." She shrugged. "Anyway, I just want to separate everything. The less Auntie Jove has to do, the better. She's already doing so much for us." She set the box down and picked up an old T-shirt that said "I Heard the Blues on the French Quarter" written across it in cracked plastic letters. It was a shirt Vea had picked up from Goodwill years ago. "Should we get rid of this, or keep it?" Ming asked.

I took the shirt from her and sat down. "Ming, I'm worried about you."

She rolled her eyes. "Don't start with that. I'm not listening to it anymore. I know the truth. I know that Auntie Jove is coming on June third. It doesn't matter to me if you're packed or not, but I'm going to be ready with my suitcase."

I eyed the locked box as she folded her shirts and pants.

"I know you don't have a suitcase of your own," she continued. "But you can stuff some of your things in here. It's not like we have that much anyway. Besides, Auntie Jove will buy us all new things."

I looked over at my sister. Her long black hair fell over her shoulders and covered much of her face, but I could see part of a smile.

"What about your art stuff?" I asked. "I don't see it anywhere."

"What art stuff?"

"Those special pencils Miss Paulsen gave you."

"Oh. Those." She didn't look at me. "I'll pack those later."

Now that I thought about it, I'd never seen those special pencils. I wondered if it was something she fibbed to me about, the way she fibbed about Vea to Imani and Maria.

The way she was fibbing to herself about Auntie Jove right now.

I got down on the floor next to her and picked up one of the shirts. I shook it out and laid it across my knees.

"You know . . ." I said. "If Auntie Jove doesn't come, we'll just have to save up all our money so we can go to the Land of Forgotten Girls."

"What?" she asked, without looking at me. She was busy rearranging the suitcase, probably trying to make room for my clothes.

"It's this place for girls like us. A place where nothing bad happens."

"Just for kids? No grown-ups?"

"Just for *girls*. And no grown-ups."

Ming rolled her eyes. "That's not real. Who would take care of us?"

I folded her shirt in half. "Well, there's a grown-up. But only one. A mother who takes care of all the girls. But she doesn't tell people what to do or boss anyone around. She just watches, to make sure no one breaks her arm or starves or something."

Ming looked at me.

"She just watches?" she asked. "She doesn't say anything, like 'clean your room' or 'you're a stupid little mouse'?"

"No. She just makes sure everyone's okay."

"But does she ever say any good stuff, like 'good job' or 'way to go'?"

Those were the kinds of stickers Ming's teachers put on her homework now and then.

"She doesn't have to," I said. "She says it with her eyes, and then all the girls just know."

"Just know what?"

"That they're happy and someone loves them."

Ming opened her mouth to say something, but went back to her suitcase instead.

✤ 20 ✤

Wire Cutters

Things I know to be true: It's easier to crawl through a giant hole in a fence than climb over it.

When Manny, Caroline, and I reached the junkyard the next day, we discovered an unevenly cut hole in the corner where Manny and I usually scaled the fence. Apparently we weren't the only ones who knew this was the best spot to get inside unnoticed.

"Good, now we don't have to climb over," I said as we all examined the new entryway.

"Thank God. I was kinda nervous," said Caroline. "I've never climbed a fence before."

Manny looked at her like she'd sprouted a second head. "You've never climbed a fence? What the—"

"Well, you don't have to start now," I said. I took a step toward the gaping hole. "Plus, we'll be able to push things out."

"Wait." Manny grabbed my shoulder. "If this hole is open, that means the Beast could break his chains and escape at any time."

"So? What, you think he's gonna come straight to your house? Ask around for you?"

Caroline laughed. Manny glared at her.

"I'm just saying," said Manny. "The dog could get out."

A voice came out of nowhere: "That's kinda the point."

The three of us turned. It was the girl from Piedmont Avenue, the one from Snout who'd given me Caroline's address. She was holding wire cutters.

There was a boy with her. He had a skateboard tucked under his arm. The girl's hair wasn't bleached anymore. Now it was dyed completely black.

"Hey, Rory," said Caroline. She frowned at the wire cutters. "Hey, Aiden."

"Hey," said Rory. She motioned toward Caroline's forehead. "That pinecone must have smacked you good, huh?" She glared at me and Manny.

Caroline brushed her fingertips over her stitches. "What, this? No. This is because of a boy. He leaned in to kiss me and we bumped our heads together."

Caroline and I both laughed, and once we started it was hard to stop. Manny didn't get the joke so instead of laughing, he said, "What's with the wire cutters?"

"Why do you need to know?" asked Aiden. He had cropped dark hair, damp with sweat. He was tall and lean, almost the exact opposite of Rory, who was short and strong. She also had blue eyeliner painted all around her eyes, which were the same color as Ming's—very dark, almost black.

"If you're trying to get in, you don't need to cut a hole in the fence," said Manny. "You just climb over, like me and Sol. It's not like you're gonna die or anything. But I guess you kids north of Tippet's are too good for all that."

Rory rolled her eyes. "We're not trying to get in, genius. We're trying to rescue the dog."

"Rescue the dog?" said Manny. "Blackbeard's Beast? Why'd you wanna do a stupid thing like that?"

"Have you seen that dog? He's chained to a camper all day. The chain is barely five feet long. All that man does is put food out. That's it."

"Yeah," said Manny. "So? I wouldn't want to play with that dog, either. He's like a wild animal."

"The reason he's mean is because he's chained up," said Rory. "That's why we're here. Once it gets dark and that dirty old man leaves, we're going inside to unchain him. Then we'll walk him through this hole"—she motioned toward the fence—"and bring him to the ASPCA. But I have to make sure the hole is big enough so he doesn't get hurt."

Manny snorted. "You're gonna get close enough to unchain that dog? What if he bites your face off?"

Aiden looked down at the wire cutters. I had a feeling he'd been wondering the same thing.

"Have you even seen that dog?" Rory said. "He doesn't even bark. He's harmless."

"He barked at us a couple days ago," I said. "At least I *think* he was barking at us."

"What do you mean, you think?" Rory asked.

"We couldn't really see him."

"Then how could he see you?"

"I don't know. He probably smelled us. But we definitely heard barking."

Now Aiden stepped in: "So you really don't know for sure that he was barking at you."

"Yes, we do," Manny said. He swatted my arm and nodded toward the fence hole. "C'mon, let's go."

"Oh, so *now* you wanna go through the hole

instead of climbing the fence?" said Rory. "Why not scale it? It's not like you're gonna *die* or anything."

"Whatever, Mother Teresa," said Manny, climbing through the hole.

"Hey," Rory said to me, "we're about to take off, but if you get close to the dog, do me a favor. Make sure he has water and stuff. It's hot. He shouldn't even be outside. It's over ninety degrees today, and dogs can overheat really easily. They can even have seizures and die. Sometimes they get confused and they faint. Or they can't catch their breath and they choke to death."

Great. As if I needed that on my conscience.

"We'll keep an eye out," said Caroline. "Don't worry."

"What're you guys doing in there, anyway?" asked Aiden.

"I don't really know," Caroline answered, a tinge of excitement in her voice. "I didn't even know this junkyard existed until today."

"It shouldn't exist," Rory said. "It's a trash heap."

"That's basically what a junkyard is," I said. "But you know what they say—one man's trash is another person's treasures."

Then I stepped through the hole in the fence with Caroline right behind me.

❧ 21 ❧
Junkyard City

"How do you know that girl, anyway?" Manny asked Caroline as the three of us maneuvered around a colony of steering wheels and rusty car parts.

"Everyone at Strout knows Rory," Caroline said. "She gets in trouble a lot."

"For what?" I asked.

"All kinds of stuff. Like, writing graffiti on the side of the school, talking back to the teachers, starting protests."

"Protests about what?"

Caroline shrugged. "I dunno, I guess stuff like she was doing with the dog. She's always talking about animals and the environment. She feeds the stray cats behind the school and the nuns go crazy."

"Nuns are already crazy, if you ask me," said Manny.

"No they aren't," snapped Caroline. "Well, not all of them."

I didn't know anything about animals or the environment. I definitely didn't know enough to protest anything.

I stopped behind a hill of car engines to survey the area. Manny and Caroline stopped, too.

"There are whole parts of the junkyard that we haven't explored yet," I said. "Like, over there." I pointed past the engine hill to a sun-drenched clearing of packed dirt in front of the camper, with its broken window and half-unhinged door. "We've never been to the other side before."

"Yeah, there's a reason, Sol. Because it's right in the psycho's line of vision." Manny turned back to Caroline. "Anyway, I thought the Snout was supposed to be a good school. That's what you'd think, the way everyone acts."

"It *is* a good school," she said.

Manny was right—the area on the other side of the clearing was unexplored for a reason. But what if there was something really great over there? What if there was a complete tree house—one that could somehow magically fit through a cut fence—sitting there in the shadows?

"Then why do they let that Rory girl stay, if she causes so much trouble?" Manny asked.

Manny was exhausting sometimes. Why were they jabbering about Rory whatshername when they should be helping me find what I was looking for? Whatever that was.

"She's nice," said Caroline, softly.

"She didn't seem very 'nice' to me."

"Well, she's not nice-nice, like in a sweet way."

Manny snorted. "Is there another way to be nice?"

"Sure," said Caroline. "There are lots of ways."

"Okay, okay," I snapped, turning to face them. "I think we should split up. We'll have better luck finding stuff that way."

"Good idea!" said Caroline, antsy with anticipation. You'd have thought we were robbing a bank, the way she was acting. "I'll start with the unexplored area."

She stepped forward and around the engine hill purposefully, until she remembered the Beast. Then she stopped, peered over—presumably to make sure the dog wasn't barreling toward her—and continued on into the clearing. The Beast picked up his head and perked his ears, but didn't do much else.

"Jeez," Manny said. His eyes darted from Caroline to the Beast. "She's walking in front of the dog. She's not even trying to hide. What if Blackbeard sees her? I told you, Sol. It was bad news for her to come along."

She doesn't know anything about—hey, what's this?"

I expected to find him pointing at a fantastic buried treasure—something that was right in front of us all this while, something we'd missed. But instead he was looking at my bracelet.

"What?" I said, crossing my arms.

"You know what. That bracelet."

"It's a bracelet, Einstein. Obviously."

"Where'd you get it?"

To be honest, I would've told him the whole story, if it weren't for his tone of voice. He sounded angry, like he *deserved* an explanation. And I didn't have to explain anything. Not if I didn't want to.

"None of your business," I said.

"Is it from a guy?"

I sighed. Now wasn't the time to talk about my bracelet. Luckily, the conversation ended there because Caroline started calling to us, saying, "I found something! Something good!" I could barely see a glimpse of her head from the massive pile of ripped-up restaurant booths and tilted boat motors. There's no telling what she was looking at.

"It's in good shape!" she called.

"Casper's gonna get us busted," Manny said.

"No, she won't," I said, even though I had my eyes on the camper. Had she hollered too loud? Did Blackbeard hear? "Let's go check it out."

Manny shook his head. "Uh-uh. No way. I'm not gettin' my throat eaten open."

I rolled my eyes. "Fine. But whatever it is—if it's something good—you're gonna help us carry it back the way we came."

I stepped away from a lopsided stack of old chairs and into the clearing. I didn't mind that Manny was staying behind. He was starting to get *under my crawl*, as Miss Moss, my English teacher, would say.

I walked into the open sun.

When you're someplace you're not supposed to be, your body knows it. The tips of my fingers and toes buzzed as I stepped into the open area. I could practically feel the pellet from Blackbeard's gun lodging itself in my hip. Worse yet, the Beast's eyes were on me. But I had to see what Caroline found, even if it meant being threatened by Blackbeard and the Beast. When you put yourself on the line, you have to decide if what you'll get is worth what you'll risk.

There's a story about Blackbeard. They say he has bodies buried under the crushed engines and glass bottles. Someone once told me that their cousin's friend bought an old refrigerator from Blackbeard and found bagged heads inside. They say he only kept the heads because he fed the bodies to the Beast. Rory must've been half crazy to want to rescue that dog. I saw long strings of slobber slide down his jowls. His pink tongue looked as big as my head. His body heaved as he panted. When he stood on all fours and stretched, I flinched.

I'd been watching the Beast so closely, with every nerve in my body shaking, that I didn't even realize I'd reached the other end of the clearing until the toe of my sneaker hit a narrow and unsteady tower of dented and useless serving trays. They wavered, but didn't fall.

Caroline was moving old crates, glass jugs, and filthy tabletops off a boat. She unearthed it like an archaeologist and pretty soon, there it was. Not a sailboat exactly. More like a canoe that only fit two people. It looked like it may have been green at one time, but most of the green paint had chipped away. Some of the wood was rotten; we didn't try to get in it. Even though it still had the slats for people to sit on, they didn't seem very sturdy. One of the slats was split and bowed. There were a bunch of little bugs scurrying around in the belly of the canoe, too. Spiders, maybe. It was hard to tell.

"This isn't in bad shape," Caroline said.

"It looks awful," I said, surprised. "No one can even get in it."

"Not right now, but we can fix it up." She stood and tilted her head left and right, like she was examining what could be. "It wouldn't take much work."

"Do you know how to do any of that stuff?"

"No."

"Me neither."

"What about Manny?"

"He'll act like he can do something, but he can't."

Caroline giggled. We turned to see what he was up to, but he wasn't there.

"Where'd he go?" Caroline asked.

"I don't know. Probably looking at stuff."

I cupped my hands around my mouth and called his name as loudly as I could without being too loud. "Manny! Manny!"

In the next second, two things happened: Manny appeared from between some rusty car doors and the Beast's chain rattled loudly. I darted forward and peeked into the clearing. The camper door had opened halfway and the Beast was facing it. He barked. A deep, deep bark. Manny cursed. Caroline ran up behind me, brushing the tower of serving trays along the way. They clamored down in a loud, clashing cascade, like a hundred cymbals falling on top of one another.

The door to the camper swung open all the way.

Blackbeard.

He looked right at me. Pointed a meaty finger my way. "Hey! Hey!"

Manny took off running. Long gone.

The Beast barked and jumped.

The chain rattled.

I pushed Caroline in front of me. "Run! Run!"

My feet stayed where they were, even as Caroline flew past me in a wave of soft white hair.

✖ 22 ✖
The Lair

Things I know to be true: It's not easy for three fugitives to escape one pellet gun. The shooter will chase you. The shooter—especially if he's angry—won't let all three of you get away. He'll fire and fire until something happens. He won't stop until he's captured at least one of you. And that person would have to be me. If it hadn't been me, it would have been Caroline. No one can beat Manny in an escape. It's like he was born to run. This was Caroline's first time at the junkyard; she didn't know her way around. And what would she have done if she reached a fence without a hole? She'd never even climbed one before. And when you're scaling a fence to get away, you can't think about it, not even for a second. You have to be swift and go.

And how would her mother have reacted when Blackbeard called and said her daughter was south of Tippet's in a junkyard with a pellet in her shoulder to go along with her stitches? I couldn't imagine that a mother who bought fancy candles and shiny bicycles would be too thrilled about her daughter wandering through a land of greasy hubcaps, especially after she just got pelted by a pinecone. Just imagine what kind of trouble Caroline would be in.

So, I let Blackbeard catch me. He grabbed me by the back of my sweaty shirt and pushed me toward his camper of death.

"You're not goin' nowheres," he said.

I held my breath. This was it. I was never to

be seen again. I could hear the news reports now: *Soledad Madrid was last seen standing near a fallen tower of serving trays.*

I clambered up the unsteady steps to the open camper. He shoved me inside and slammed the door behind him. Then he pointed to a fold-out chair against a wall, next to a desk buried in papers.

"Sit," he said.

I sat.

Blackbeard's lair wasn't what I expected. There was no giant oven for cooking children. No hatchets to chop off heads. No gun rack for all his weaponry. Just a cramped and untidy camper. And it wasn't even as messy as you might think.

Blackbeard shuffled papers around on his desk, which was littered with Styrofoam coffee cups, three ancient keyboards, and two outdated computer monitors covered in a film of dust. He was muttering, but I couldn't understand what he was saying. His cheeks and forehead were red and glistening. His beard was dark and sweaty. His hands were lined with grease.

To my left was a small kitchenette with a mini fridge. It was fairly clean, all things considered. To my right was a closet and bathroom. There were stacks of books in corners and two big bags of dog food on the floor by my feet.

"Do you live here?" I asked.

"Live here?" he grunted, still moving the papers. "No, I don't live here. I live in Kenner."

That's not far from Giverny.

"Do you own this place?"

"What? Yeah, yeah . . ."

"What are you looking for?" Part of me didn't want to know.

"My *phone*, little girl. My phone. To call the police. I'm tired of you wetbacks breakin' in here."

"I'm not Mexican." *And if you call my friend a wetback, I'll hit you with this bag of dog chow.*

Blackbeard didn't seem to care whether or not

I was Mexican. He just kept moving things around and cursing under his breath. At least I knew he was calling the police and not sawing me to pieces.

I looked around some more. There was a bookshelf against the opposite wall. It was filled with glass bottles. Nothing special, it seemed. Not at first. But then I leaned forward—without getting out of my chair—and looked closer.

The bottles weren't dirty. They were perfectly clean, like they'd been wiped with Windex a hundred times. And there was something inside each of them. Something small. Like a message in a bottle, but they weren't messages.

The words came out before I could stop them: "Hey, what're those?"

"What're what?"

I pointed at the bottles. "Those."

He looked at the bookshelf and cleared his throat. "What, those? Just junk, that's all. Like everything else."

I walked over to the bookshelf.

It didn't look like junk to me.

Inside each bottle was a miniature scene. One had sand at the bottom, and a tiny little plastic family making a sand castle. Another one was a boat, sailing on waves of crystal-blue marbles. Here was a flowerbed. There was a genie on a pile of pillows. Everywhere I looked was a new story, trapped in glass. At least a dozen, maybe more.

"Wow," I said. "Where'd you get these?"

"I made 'em," he replied.

"Made them? How?"

He came from around the desk and stood next to me, grumbling to himself all the way. He smelled like rusty steel.

"That was the first one I made," he said, pointing to the beach scene. His fingernail was so dirty it was completely black.

"How'd you get the little people inside?"

"That's top secret, I'm afraid."

"What about that one, with the sailboat? How'd you get it to fit in there?"

"Like I said, top secret. An artist never reveals his secrets."

"I thought that was just magicians."

"Same thing."

I always thought of artists as wearing berets and sipping tiny cups of coffee with their pinkie fingers in the air, not sweaty men with stinky beards who looked and smelled like a junkyard.

"My little sister would love these," I said.

The Beast's chain rattled outside.

"Well, I don't show 'em off too much," Blackbeard mumbled "Just a hobby. You know."

The chain rattled again.

"Can I ask you a question, sir?" I said.

"I got a feeling you'll ask no matter what. So, go ahead."

"How come you keep your dog chained up?"

"So he don't run off. Why else?"

"Did you know that dogs can have seizures in hot weather? They get really thirsty. They're not supposed to be outside when it's hot, and it's always hot. Plus, it's not good to keep them chained up. It makes them mean."

"I want him to be mean. That's the point."

I shrugged. "I just wanted to let you know. It can't be easy out in the heat. Maybe you can bring him inside now and then. Not all the time, but sometimes. And you always have to make sure he has plenty of water."

"What're you, some kinda kid veterinarian?"

I shrugged. We stood there in silence staring at the bookshelf for what seemed like forever. But I didn't mind. Each bottle was completely different and I couldn't figure out how he was able to set up the little scenes inside. I racked my brain. Did he build the bottle around them? No, that couldn't be right—these were old glass bottles, just like the ones in the junkyard. Did he push everything inside until it fit? Maybe—but then how was he able to get them to sit up straight and look like stories, instead of random trash shoved into a bottle?

"I can't figure out how you did it," I said.

"That's what makes it interesting," he replied. He crossed his arms and tucked his hands under his armpits. "What were you kids doin' in my junkyard, anyway?"

"Looking for something."

"Looking for what?"

"I don't know. Anything. We saw an old rowboat. That's what we were looking at when you caught me." Even though he didn't really catch me. I surrendered.

"What you want with that old rowboat?"

"I was gonna fix it up."

"You better know what you're doin' before you take an old rowboat from my junkyard out to the water or you'll drown, sure as I'm standing here."

I thought of Amelia. Her hair flowing in the water behind her. My mother's high-pitched scream.

"We weren't going to take it on the water," I said, swallowing away the memory. "I was going to restore it for my little sister, Ming."

"What kinda name is 'Ming'?"

"Short for Dominga. Just like my name is Sol, short for Soledad." I looked at him. "What's your name, anyway?" It was hard to believe he had a name other than Blackbeard.

"My name?" He huffed. "Mean Junkyard Owner."

"I guess your parents didn't really give you much of a choice, huh?"

Blackbeard paused for a second, then laughed. He had a good laugh. The way Santa Claus might sound if he lived in a trash heap instead of the North Pole.

When he finished laughing, he said, "Whatcha gonna restore it for, if you don't wanna take it to the water?"

When I was little my mom lined up the kitchen chairs and pretended we were on a sailboat. I wanted something like that for Ming. A place she could go that's just for her. I wanted to build her a tree house, but there aren't any trees at the Tower.

But I didn't tell him that.

"I don't know," I said. "It was stupid."

I stared at the family in the glass bottle, building a sand castle. Mom, Dad, and two daughters. They even had a little dog with them. Everyone was smiling. Painted-on smiles. Permanent. I wished I could live in there with them.

"Tell you what," Blackbeard said. "You bring me something good for my junkyard—like a trade—and we'll call it even. I won't call the police and I'll give you the old rowboat, if you promise not to take it out on the water."

"Promise."

"I'll even tell you how I got the little people inside the bottles. Deal?" He stuck out his beefy hand. His fingers were short and fat, like sausages, and felt rough and scratchy.

"Deal," I said.

❧ 23 ❧

Fairy Tale

Manny was sitting on the stoop of the Tower when I got back. He hopped up when he saw me.

"I thought you got arrested or something, or maybe he kidnapped you and locked you in a closet," he said. He took off his cap and put it on again, the way he does when he's nervous. "I figured if Vea came out, I'd know one way or another if he called the cops or not. What *happened*?"

I sat on the stoop. He sat down next to me, fidgety and anxious.

"I told Casper to go home and we'd fill her in later," he said. He was so hyped up, he was talking fifty miles a minute. "We thought you were right behind us, then when she saw that you got nabbed, she flipped out and she—"

"Don't call her that."

"Don't call her what?"

"Casper."

"You're the one who came up with it."

"I know. But it's mean."

"Excuse me, Miss High-and-Mighty."

"How would you like it if she called you a wetback?"

"That's different." His voice was flat now. "That's, like, a *racial slur.*"

"It's the same thing."

"No, it's not."

"Yes, it is."

"No, it's—" He sighed. Stared off at the field across the street, the one with all the tires. "Sol, can I ask you something?"

"Go ahead."

He took a deep breath. "Where'd you get that bracelet? Did you get it from a guy?"

"After everything that just happened, you wanna talk about my bracelet?"

"No."

"Then why'd you ask?"

"Because you're being all mysterious about it, which makes me think it's from a guy."

"So what if it is? What are you, jealous or something?"

"I'm not jealous," he snapped.

"Then why do you care?"

"I just . . ." He shrugged. "I don't know. I guess I've just been thinking about you and . . . I don't know . . ." He shrugged again. "I thought you might see me as more than a friend?" He said it as a question, not a statement.

There were girls at Leo who sometimes went out with boys they didn't like just because there was no one better, or maybe they thought they would eventually start to like the guy, or just because they wanted to have a date to a dance or something. I didn't want to be like that.

"I don't have time to think about that stuff, Manny," I said. "I'm trying to figure out a way to get out of here with Ming."

Manny bit the inside of his cheek and leaned his head back the way he does when he's embarrassed, upset, or both, and trying to figure out what to say next.

"I hate to tell you this, Sol," he said, looking at me again. "But you won't get out of here. You're twelve years old. What are you gonna do, run away?"

I sat up straight. "Maybe."

"You've never even driven a car," he added. "What're you gonna do, get on a bus so some dude like Blackbeard can kidnap both of you?"

I didn't answer. I thought about the little family in the bottle.

He stood up. Brushed the dirt from the back of his pants. "You're living in a fairy tale, Sol. You really are." He practically sprinted off.

"If that's true," I called out, "when does the good stuff start?"

❧ 24 ❧
Fair Swap

Things I know to be true: There is something very strange about the Fair Swap Pawn Shop. It's like the junkyard, except the junk is up on shelves with price tags dangling off it. There's something sad about it, too. When you walk down the aisles, you think of all the people who have come in to sell little pieces of their lives—a diamond ring, an old worn chair, a favorite dress. It even smells like a place where people have sold off life's important things. Last summer Manny and

I spent a lot of time in the Fair Swap looking around, but the owner didn't like us much. There is a big sign that says "Do Not Move Items," but one afternoon— our last time in there—I grabbed a rusty dagger from the shelf and pretended to slay dragons with it, then Manny took down a panel of stained glass and used it as a shield. While we were fake fighting, we knocked over some ancient railroad signal and the man told us not to come back.

When I walked into the Fair Swap with Ming, I was relieved to see that the man behind the counter wasn't the same man who kicked me and Manny out. It was a younger guy, tall and skinny. He came around from behind the display case and asked if we needed any help. He looked at us suspiciously, like we were there to steal.

"I was wondering if you could tell me how much something is worth?" I said.

"You have to be eighteen to pawn," he said. "Come back with your mother."

"We don't have one," said Ming.

The man frowned. I put my hand on Ming's shoulder.

"I just want to know how much something is worth." I lifted my arm to show him the bracelet. "This."

He took my wrist and brought it closer. His skin was rough.

"All right," he said, walking around the display case. "Come here."

We followed him to the case, which was full of jewelry—some old, some new—on faded velvet.

"I'm no expert, but I'll take it to the back so my uncle can give it a look-see," the skinny guy said, tilting his head toward a closed curtain that must have opened to a back room. I wondered if his uncle was the man who didn't like me and Manny. "Well? Hand it over." He opened his hand. I hesitated. "Don't worry, kid," he said. "I'm not gonna steal it."

After I gave him the bracelet and he disappeared

behind the ratty curtain, Ming got on her tiptoes and leaned close to the glass, so close that her nose almost touched it, even though there was a big sign that said "Do Not Lean On, Or Touch, Glass." Pawn shops have a lot of rules about touching and moving things.

Ming pressed her index finger against the case. "Look at that green one. It's my favorite."

The ring was gold with a bright gem sitting on top of it. It was green like the color of the first bright leaves of spring. I had no idea if it was a real emerald or not, but the price tag said $119, so I guessed that it must be.

"That's an emerald," I said.

"Like Emerald City in *Wizard of Oz*?"

"Yeah, only better."

"How could it be better?"

"Because Emerald City isn't real, and this ring is." I leaned closer. "Emeralds like this one are made to bring good luck to whoever wears them. Emeralds have magical powers, you know. You can't go wrong if you're wearing an emerald." I nodded matter-of-factly.

"They're so lucky that every girl gets one when she arrives in the Land of Forgotten Girls. The mother there recognizes her girls by the exact shade of their emeralds. That's just one more reason why I hope we can go there one day."

Ming leaned so close to the glass that it fogged when she talked.

"How come she doesn't recognize their faces?" she asked.

"Oh, she does. Mother Hush recognizes their faces *and* their emeralds."

"Mother Hush?"

"That's her name."

"Kinda like Mother Goose."

"Yeah, but way better."

When the curtain opened, Ming flattened her feet and took a step back, but her finger had left a big round print on the glass. If the skinny man noticed, he didn't seem to care. He handed me the bracelet.

"A hundred dollars, give or take," he said as I clasped it on my wrist.

Ming's eyes widened. "A hundred dollars! Sol, you're rich!"

A hundred dollars. That seemed like a lot of money for Mrs. Yeung to hand over. She probably didn't know how much it was worth because she had so much stuff in her apartment.

"Need anything else?" the skinny guy said.

I shook my head.

"Have a good summer, then." His face was friendlier than it was when we'd walked in.

"Oh, we will," said Ming. "Our aunt is coming to pick us up on June third and take us away from this place. We're going to see all kinds of great, new things and have all kinds of wonderful adventures."

The man smiled. I put my arm around Ming and guided her toward the door.

"Take care of your big sister, then," the man said.

I leaned toward Ming. "You sure have become a chatterbox."

The bell over the door jingled as we walked out.

Ming shrugged. "Well, how else will I talk to Auntie Jove?"

I didn't answer. I looked at my bracelet instead. I'd never had anything worth a hundred dollars before. I'd better be sure to hide it from Vea.

The sun was so bright that we both had to squint. The sidewalk in front of Fair Swap was cracked and pushed up in all different places, so you really had to pay attention. Ming stumbled a little bit and I had to grab the back of her shirt.

"Watch where you step," I said.

For the next block she never took her eyes off the sidewalk. She dodged another crack and said, "Sol—can I ask you a question?"

"As long as it's not about Auntie Jove or Amelia."

"It's not."

"Okay, then."

"Did Mrs. Yeung really give you that bracelet?"

"Yeah. Why would I make that up?"

"I thought maybe Manny gave it to you and you didn't want to tell me."

"I would tell you if he did. Besides, why would he do a thing like that?"

"Because he likes you."

"Maybe," I said. "But he doesn't have any money so he wouldn't be able to give me a bracelet."

"Would you like him if he had money?"

"No. He's my best friend. I only like him as a friend."

"What's the difference?"

"I don't know."

"Then how do you know that you only like him as a friend?"

"I just do."

"Do you think our father only liked Vea as a friend and that's why he never came back?"

I swallowed. "Maybe. It's hard to believe, though."

"Why is it hard to believe?"

"It's hard to believe anyone would like Vea as a friend."

She stumbled on another crack and I caught her again.

"What do you think Vea was like when she was a kid?" Ming asked.

I was about to say *evil*, but then I really thought about it. I tried to imagine Vea as a little girl like Ming, or an almost-teenager like me. It was hard to picture her without cigarettes or thorny words or wrinkles around her black eyes. It felt really strange to think of her as a little kid. I wondered if her parents were mean to her, or if she even had real parents.

"I don't know," I said.

"I bet she was mean even when she was little," said Ming. "I bet she was even meaner than Brandy Anderson."

"Who's Brandy Anderson?"

Ming didn't answer right away, but then she said, "This big, mean, ugly girl at my school."

"How is she mean?"

"She just is," said Ming. "She likes to mess with people. That's why I like to get into the tree house before anyone else."

I thought of Ming, scurrying up the ladder of a tree house. I pictured her pushing herself against its walls, hoping to disappear.

Amelia came out of corners. Ming hid in them. Where did that leave me? Unable to protect either of them, that's where.

"What's she look like?" I asked. Maybe I'd have a talk with this girl if I ever saw her around.

Ming scratched a mosquito bite just above her knobby elbow. "I told you. Big, mean, and ugly." She stretched her arm up as high as she could over her head. "Like, this tall! And she's in my grade. Can you believe?"

"Maybe she's under an evil spell, like the Beast in *Beauty and the Beast.*"

"Or maybe she'll grow and grow, like a beanstalk."

"Maybe she comes from a planet where everyone is eight feet tall."

"Maybe she ate a piece of a mushroom and she's never been able to find the other half to shrink to normal size."

"Maybe the meaner she gets, the taller she gets."

Ming thought about that for a second. "No, that can't be true."

"Why not?"

"Because if that were true, she'd be a lot taller than she is now."

I laughed.

"Maybe I should be meaner," said Ming. "Then I could grow a little bit and not be so mousy."

I turned one of the pearls of my bracelet between my fingers. "There's nothing wrong with being a mouse. Mice are strong. There's even a story about a mouse that saved the life of a lion. Mama used to tell it to me when I was little. You wanna hear it?"

She nodded.

"One day this enormous lion got very hungry, so he caught a mouse for dinner. He opened his mouth wide, stuck out his slobbery, disgusting tongue, and dangled the little mouse over his sharp teeth. But the mouse said, 'Lion, if you let me live, I promise I'll never forget it, and I'll find a way to repay you.' The lion laughed so hard that he roared. 'How could a mouse ever do anything for *me*? I'm even bigger than Brandy Anderson!'"

Ming laughed. A beat-up car drove by with booming music, but she kept her eyes on me.

I continued, "The lion was so amused by the mouse's promise that he let him go, and he laughed the whole time as the mouse disappeared into the trees. A few weeks passed. He'd forgotten all about the mouse. He was walking along, minding his own business, when *whack*!"—I slapped my hands together—"he got caught in a hunter's net! He was all twisted up in there, very uncomfortable, and there was no way out. He knew that the hunters would come for him pretty soon and that would be the end of Mr. Lion. Until—"

"—the mouse showed up!"

Someone had chucked a plastic water bottle in the sidewalk. Ming kicked it in mock celebration, then picked it up to throw away later.

"Yep," I said. "The mouse showed up and said, 'Well, Lion, it's time for me to return that favor I owe you.' And the mouse chewed all the way through the net until the lion was free. The end."

Ming nodded, satisfied. "So I guess there *is* something worse than being mousy."

"Yep," I said. "Like being a fire-breathing dragon in dirty pink slippers."

❧ 25 ❧
Sister Ribbons

My mother once told me that sisters were bound by invisible ribbons, and these ribbons held them together until the end of time, no matter what. She said that was why some sisters could tell when the other was in trouble.

When Amelia died, I felt like something deep in my heart was broken, and it wasn't just because it was my fault she died. My mother said it wasn't, but I knew better. If only I had come out from behind the tree the first time my mother called my name, she would've never turned away. All it took was that one moment for the river to steal my sister.

For weeks after Amelia died I lay in bed, listening to the steady buzz of the mosquitos, and imagined that I had a ribbon in my hand, dangling in the air, waiting for Amelia to catch onto it, even though she never did. That's what it feels like when your sister dies: like you're waiting for something, but you don't know what, or you're looking for something that you can never find, only you're not really looking; you're just drifting. It wasn't the same with my mother. When she died, I felt like my whole spirit had been cracked in two, and even though I could be put back together, I would never be the same. But when Amelia died, I felt lost, like I would spend my whole life searching for her.

One of Vea's favorite things to say about me was that I was *a selfish little kano*. And she's right. I *am* selfish. I didn't come out from my hiding place because I wanted my mother to keep searching for me. I wanted to see how hard she'd look.

At Amelia's funeral everyone talked about what a wonderful girl she was, and they were right. She was wonderful, just like our mother. And every time someone hugged me, I wondered if they were thinking the same thing I was: *It should have been you, Sol. It should have been you.*

Amelia showed up again and again when I needed her. The first time Vea squeezed my nose and spit in my hair. That time I cheated on a test and felt really bad about it. The first time I slept in our new room in the Tower. And now—as Ming slept beside me, the night of our visit to Fair Swap—she visited again. Only this time her face emerged from the ceiling and hovered above, like an angel.

"I need your help," I said.

"I know," she replied. Her hair floated around her, just like it did that day.

"But first I have a question."

"And I have an answer."

I took a deep breath. "Am I imagining you?" I whispered. "Or are you real?"

"That depends," said Amelia.

"On what?"

"On what you believe to be real and true."

"What's true is that Ming needs help and I can't help her. What's true is that her closet is just a closet and Auntie Jove is just a story. That's what's true."

Amelia shrugged. It was a ghostly, watery shrug that sent her black hair swirling.

"If you say so," she said.

"What do you mean, if I say so? What's true is true and what isn't, isn't. I should've done a better job showing her the difference."

Amelia floated down, down, down from the ceiling until she was back in the corner again, staring at me with her tired eyes.

"Do you remember the day Mama took us to the market and told us the story of Salvatore the Sitaw Man?" she asked.

How unexpected. My heart emptied the way it does when you hear a nice memory from the past that you'd long forgotten. Salvatore the Sitaw Man, of course I remembered. He was very tall for a Filipino, and thin, too. His fingers were thin, his ears were thin, even his hair was thin. Every time we went to the market, he was there. He was so tall that he stood above all the other vendors. At the market, there were certain things you were sure to see: bins and bins of bright and colorful fruits and vegetables, endless throngs of people shouting and haggling over prices, and tall, tall Salvatore.

"You see that man?" Mama whispered to me one afternoon, pointing her chin toward Salvatore. One of her hands held Amelia, the other a bag of rice. Ming, as always, slept on her chest. Endless groups of people moved all around us, hollering about *pesos* this and *pesos* that.

"That tall man?" I looked toward Salvatore, who stood behind an enormous bin of *sitaw*—string beans.

"Yes, Tito Salvatore," she whispered. "He used to be a string bean."

I blurted out a laugh then slapped my hand over my mouth to stop myself. "No, he didn't!" I said once I'd calmed down.

"Oh yes, he did," Mama continued, her voice low. "Why do you think he's so tall? He made a deal with a wicked witch. He said, 'Please make me human. I'll do anything.' So, poof! She turned him human. He said, 'What do I owe you?' And she said, 'You must sell every string bean in the Philippines, and then I'll set you free.' Why else do you think he's here every day?"

My eyes grew wide. From that point on, I always watched Salvatore carefully, looking for hints of green, or for secret seeds coming out of his ears.

"I remember," I told Amelia. My heart suddenly ached for my mother.

"The story Mama told, about him being a string bean—was that the truth?"

"No. Of course not."

"So she lied?"

"Our mother was no liar."

"See?" she said, opening her arms wide. "Sometimes there's an in-between. It's good to hide in the in-between sometimes. Isn't it?"

While I was thinking of the best way to answer, she disappeared.

26

Chips and Cracks

Mrs. Yeung's bracelet was the most valuable thing I owned, but I didn't feel right about owning it. Maybe she didn't know how much it was worth. Or maybe she only gave it to me because she felt sorry for me. Maybe she expected me to sell it without a second thought.

I decided that the best thing to do was to return the bracelet or at least tell Mrs. Yeung how much it was worth. So early the next morning, while Ming and Vea were still asleep, I went to Mrs. Yeung's apartment and knocked on the door. I hoped she was already awake.

It didn't take long for Mrs. Yeung to open the door, and from the looks of things she had been awake for a while. All the lights were on, it smelled like tea, and she was wearing a knit cap, which was strange since it was so hot outside and in our building.

"Good morning, Mrs. Yeung," I said. "I came to talk to you about the bracelet."

She opened the door wide. She motioned toward the kettle of tea, but I shook my head and unclasped the bracelet.

"I went to the Fair Swap yesterday with my sister and found out how much your bracelet is worth," I said. I held it out for her. "I don't feel right about taking it. It's worth a lot of money, way more than the ten dollars I asked for. It doesn't seem right."

Her forehead creased. She looked at the bracelet,

but instead of taking it, she shook her head and pushed it back toward me.

"You don't understand, Mrs. Yeung. It's worth one hundred dollars. That's a lot of money."

She held her palms toward me and kept shaking her head. Then she held up an index finger—*wait*—and disappeared into her room. I wasn't sure what to do, so I put the bracelet back on. Maybe she didn't understand what I was saying. Maybe I should write it down. I looked around for a paper and pencil, but before I could find either, she was back. She had a framed picture in her hand, which she held up for me to see. It was an old, yellowish photo with three people in it—one short girl, one tall girl, and one in-between girl. The tall girl had a big, bright smile. One of those smiles that makes you want to smile, too. She had her arm around the littlest one. Mrs. Yeung pointed at the little girl, then at herself.

"Oh, that's you?" I said. I took the picture so I could study it closer. The little girl looked nothing like Mrs. Yeung. This girl was young and round-faced, with dimples. I squinted at her to see if there were clues that she would become Mrs. Yeung, but she just looked like a little girl. Mrs. Yeung pointed to the tall girl.

"Is that your sister?" I asked, even though I had a pretty good idea that she was. Mrs. Yeung didn't answer. She just smiled. So did I. "She looks happy," I said.

Mrs. Yeung then pointed to the girl's arm—the one that was around the little girl's shoulders—and I nearly fell over because the pearl bracelet was dangling on her wrist, right there in the picture.

"This belongs to your sister?" I handed the picture back to her. "Oh, I really can't take it, then, Mrs. Yeung." I felt weirdly panicked, like I'd stolen it right from her secret safe, which I still hadn't seen anywhere. "I don't deserve something so special." I fumbled with the clasp so I could take it off again, but she pushed my hands away and shook her head.

"Mrs. Yeung, you don't understand." I sighed. "I don't deserve this. I'm not a good sister. I try to be, but—" I swallowed and closed my eyes. "I'm not a good sister. You don't know this, but . . ." I looked at her. Her face was so old. I wondered where her sister was. I wondered if she knew about invisible ribbons. "I had another little sister, Amelia. She died," I said.

Sometimes there are certain words that make your voice crack, and you have to try really hard not to cry after saying them. When I told Mrs. Yeung about Amelia, my voice suddenly cracked and I had to press my lips together real tight to stop myself from crying. I turned away and focused on the bracelet. I thought about what kind of sister Mrs. Yeung must have had. She had a strong sister, a protector, I bet. The kind of sister who would come when her mother called. The kind of sister with a smile that said *Don't worry; I will always protect you*.

"She died because of me, because I wouldn't come out from behind the tree. My mother called my name three times. . . . She only turned away for a few seconds. . . . I should've come out. . . ."

I didn't look up at Mrs. Yeung, but I could feel her eyes on me. Thinking about how selfish I was, probably. Thinking, *What girl doesn't come when her mother calls three times?* "Ming needs help, but there's nothing I can do. When Auntie Jove doesn't come, I don't know what'll happen. Vea will probably stick her with thorns."

Mrs. Yeung propped the old photo on the corner of her kitchen counter and turned to me.

"I can't even give her a tree house," I said. I blurted it out. And my voice cracked again, but not just my voice. Something deep inside me, too.

I thought about Amelia and Ming. I even thought about Manny and the way he looked at me when I told him he was only my friend. I thought about the way the pinecone made Caroline's head bleed, and how she touched her stitches and tried to make me feel better about it. I thought of my father, the way he looked the last time I saw him, and how later I would realize that maybe he was thinking, even way back then, that he would never return. I thought of the cigarette burning into Mr. Elephant's head and how he used to flop over Ming's arm when she carried him around. I thought about my mother, how she took us on imaginary sails around the world and made up tales about Auntie Jove. I thought of the way Vea looked at me, like I was a dirty piece of garbage that she couldn't take out.

Sad thoughts have a way of carrying you away, like you're in a different place, so I forgot I was standing in front of Mrs. Yeung's closed door. I felt like I was alone in the universe, standing on an island surrounded by water, or maybe trapped in a high tower like Rapunzel. I forgot someone else was with me until Mrs. Yeung gently pulled at my hands. I was embarrassed, really embarrassed, like I'd just committed a grave sin, even if I wasn't sure what it was.

I figured she was going to push me out the door, but instead she started writing on the back of my hand with a pen. When she finished, she looked at me and pointed to what she'd written:

希望

I took a good, deep breath.

"I don't know what this means, Mrs. Yeung," I said. My voice sounded strange. Like it didn't belong to me.

She patted my hand, then did something else that I didn't expect: she kissed me on the forehead, just like my mother used to do. Then she scooped up her picture and carried it back into her bedroom, and somehow I knew it was time for me to go.

✖ 27 ✖
Apartment Two

I stood in the shadowy hallway, staring at the back of my hand, for what felt like a lifetime. I thought of a hundred things Mrs. Yeung may have written: *You're a fool, Sol Madrid; You should've come out of that coconut tree, little girl; You may never polish my jewels again.* Or maybe it was something that would help me, some message to stop the cracking of my soul. The combination to her safe. The secret to her inheritance, maybe. Or just a simple phrase: Everything will be all right, I promise.

The only way I would ever know was to ask someone. But who did I know who spoke Mrs. Yeung's language and also spoke English?

No one.

Unless—

I looked away from my hand and toward the closed door of apartment two. Someone was home; that much was clear. Someone was always home at the Langs and Kwoks—there were so many of them living inside those tiny apartments.

I walked up to the door and knocked, but it sounded very loud inside and no one came right away. So I knocked harder. Then I heard shouting that I couldn't understand and the door swung open. A man stood there—I couldn't tell how old he was, only that he was a grown-up—and his face was knotted and irritated, as if he was in the middle of a super-important task. I caught a glimpse of the living room behind him. It didn't look as crowded as I would've expected, but their couch and chair looked ratty and mismatched. I wondered if their furniture came with the apartment, like ours.

"I'm looking for . . . um . . ." Duh. I just realized I had no idea what the woman's name was. "The lady with the hairbun."

The man stared at me. It was clear he had no idea what I was saying, so I curled my hand in a ball and tapped it against the nape of my neck.

"Hairbun?" I said. "Lang? Hairbun Lang?"

Hairbun Lang. Nice.

The man's face relaxed but didn't exactly turn friendly. He walked off with the door open, hollering.

I tapped my fingers against my legs. It felt weird being in front of yet another new door, but not as weird as it must have looked to Vea, who walked in through the lobby at that moment holding two Stop-N-Go bags. She must've snagged a bunch of leftovers this time. Or else she bought a few extras. Every now and then she surprised us with a bag of chips or something. You'd have thought she brought in bars of silver, the way she'd act about it.

"What're you doing?" she asked me, charging right over like an angry bull.

"None of your business."

She stood next to me and craned her neck around the sliver of door that was still open. We could hear the knotty-faced man.

"What's going on?" Vea lowered her voice. The smell of fried fish wafted up from the bags. "You get in trouble with these people?"

"No. I just have to ask Hairbun Lang a question."

"Who?"

But then she appeared in the doorway. Hair in a bun, wearing her casino uniform. Only her name wasn't Hairbun Lang. According to her name tag, it was June.

June looked me up and down, then Vea.

I tacked on my best smile, but it didn't fool her one bit.

"What do you want?" she said.

"Do you speak English?" I asked—a stupid question, considering she'd just spoken it.

"Better than you," she snapped.

"And can you read this?" I held up the back of my hand.

"What're you, my first-grade reading teacher? I'm taking some kinda spelling quiz from a ten-year-old?"

"I'm twelve." I lifted my hand higher. "I just want to know what this means, that's all."

June snatched my fingers toward her and shot daggers at whatever Mrs. Yeung had written there. I wondered if she'd be friendlier if her bun wasn't so tight.

"You work at the casino?" said Vea.

June let go of my hand and now focused on Vea. Great.

"Yeah," said June. "So?"

"So I've been trying to get a job there for a year. They hiring?"

"They're always hiring." She eyed Vea some more, like she was sizing her up. "They've got a cage cashier job open, but just part-time."

"They don't hire Filipinos," said Vea. She left out the part about all the jobs going to the Chinese.

"They don't care if you're Filipino or black or Mexican or what, as long as you show up and count the money," said June.

Mrs. Yeung's ink burned through my skin.

"Let's go," Vea said to me. She grabbed my shirtsleeve. "Time for dinner." She thanked June without a hint of enthusiasm.

"Wait, wait!" I said as June began to shut the door and Vea yanked me toward apartment four. "Do you know what it says on my hand?"

June stuck her head into the dimly lit hallway.

"It says 'hope'!" she called, just before she slammed the door.

28

Hummingbird

I stayed wide awake long after Vea and Ming had fallen asleep. I couldn't get the thought of finding Mr. Elephant out of my head. I stared at the ceiling, so deep in my thoughts that I didn't move a muscle. When Amelia appeared in the corner, I told her, "There is only one thing that could make Ming happier than Auntie Jove. Mr. Elephant. Do you think I can find him?" She gave a watery shrug, but said nothing else.

I just lay there like stone, staring and thinking

and staring and thinking. And then I thought: What am I waiting for? No need to waste another second. I could search for him. I would be quiet as a mouse. Stealthy, like a cat burglar. It wouldn't take me long, after all. Apartment four wasn't very big. I could even search Vea's room, if I was quiet enough.

I decided to search the simplest, least likely place first—our room—to get some practice.

I knelt on the floor and looked underneath the bed. I knew Mr. Elephant wouldn't be there, but when you search for something, you have to search everywhere. Leave no stone unturned.

I saw crumpled paper. Ming's suitcase. A few bundled-up T-shirts that I'd forgotten about. Two dusty bouncy balls from an old gum ball machine that Tippet's used to have.

And Ming's letter box.

I pulled it out and stared at it in the dark, with the sound of Ming's restful breathing above me. She hadn't moved, hadn't heard me. She didn't hear me when I yanked on the lock. Not even when I lifted the box to my ear and shook it.

Ming had locked it tight.

She didn't even wake up when I broke it.

I knew it was wrong. When I heard the lock crack against the bedpost, a piece of me cracked with it. But I had to know. Even if I already did.

The hinge was attached by only one tiny screw. There would be no way to cover up my crime. But that didn't matter now.

I opened the lid.

The box was empty.

I picked the now-useless lock off the carpet and put it inside, where the letter should have been. Then I closed the box—slowly, slowly—and returned it to its hiding place under the bed.

I'd found what I expected to find: nothing. But sometimes what you expect and what you want are two very different things. I could've cried. But I had a job to do.

I tried to remember everything Manny had said, about how to go through a house without being heard.

You need a plan. Almost like a map, so you know exactly what you're gonna do when you get in there.

First, I would search the closet in the hallway. Next, Vea's room, followed by the living room. I would end with the kitchen. Basically, I would work my way up from the back of the apartment to the front.

Then, once it's go time, you should dress in black so you blend in with the dark.

All I had was an old black T-shirt. That would have to do. I rummaged through the closet quietly. I found the shirt stuffed in the back next to that stupid license plate I had picked up at the junkyard.

I put it on, then stood up. Slowly.

Once you're all dressed and you've got your plan all mapped out, you go inside. But you can't walk like you normally do....You've got to walk on your toes first, then ease back on your heels.

I practiced around the room, just like he'd shown me, and he was right—I barely made a sound. I decided that I was a goblet thief, about to break into the world's largest castle. The Queen of the Cups had ordered me to steal the most valuable goblet in the world, which had fallen into the hands of her greatest enemy, the Witch Head.

Maybe it was stupid, but I didn't care. The best thing about having a mind is that it's invisible—you can think whatever you want, even if it's childish, and it doesn't matter. Your thoughts belong to you, and only you.

So that's what I was: A goblet thief.

And beyond my bedroom door was the biggest goblet-holding castle in the world.

I turned our doorknob—slowly, applying pressure with my free hand where the door met the frame, just like Manny had said—and tilted my ear toward the hallway, trying to make out any sounds of movement. I lifted my nose, too. Did I smell cigarette smoke?

No.

Nothing.

I stepped out. The castle was empty, quiet and motionless, so I listened. *You've gotta be listening at all times. Like, on high-high alert.* I stealth-walked toward the closet in the hallway and stealth-opened the door. Neatly folded towels, linens (the same ones we'd had since we moved from the Philippines), two rolls of toilet paper (the thin kind that barely does any good), and an old cracked plastic laundry basket that was there when we moved in. The basket was so broken that it couldn't even be used, but for some reason it was still sitting there.

No Mr. Elephant.

I couldn't remember the last time I'd been in Vea's room, but if Mr. Elephant was hidden anywhere, it would be there. That's where I would keep it if I were her.

Her door opened easily, but it creaked. You never notice the sounds a place makes until it's the only sound in the world. *Creeeak.* I once read that a hummingbird's heart beat more than a thousand times a minute. I was like a hummingbird now, listening to the *creeeeak*.

Once the door was open, I waited, expecting Vea to emerge from her bed like a vampire rising from its tomb. But there was no movement. Only light streaming in from the streetlamps and the moon.

I stayed on the balls of my feet and walked in.

The room smelled like an ashtray. Her bed was in the corner. The outline of her rail-thin body was barely noticeable under the blanket. She breathed deeply and made a weird sound when she slept—not exactly a snore, but something like it.

Her grubby pink slippers were on the floor next to the bed. An alarm clock glowed on the nightstand—one-fifteen, June second. In the opposite corner were three laundry baskets in a row, full of clothes. She never put her clothes away. She kept them in the baskets and took what she needed as she went along. She didn't have a dresser, and I guess she didn't see the point of hanging T-shirts in the closet.

I walked toward the laundry baskets. Stealthy. Halfway there, I heard something and stopped. *If you hear something, you stop where you are and stand very still. Never take off running or anything stupid like that. You only move if you're able to hide.* I wasn't able to hide—I was standing basically in the middle of her bedroom—so I froze and crouched and turned into a hummingbird again. A second later, I heard Vea's snore-like exhale, and I began to pick through the clothes as silently as possible. It would have been a good place to hide Mr. Elephant, but he wasn't there.

I went to her closet and opened the door. It creaked a little, but not enough to rustle the Witch Head. Inside were more clothes, most of them on the floor, and no Mr. Elephant. I saw three shoeboxes on the closet shelf. They were full of junk, like loose change, old photos, and pencils. One of the photos was a picture of Vea. Even though she was much younger, I could tell it was her. She was smiling and holding up bright blue *halo-halo*—a type of Filipino shaved ice—for whoever took the picture. It reminded me of how Manny's mouth looked that day he told me about the girls he kissed.

I turned the picture over. *Vea, 11*, it said.

I looked at the lump under the blankets and put the picture back in the shoebox. I pulled out something else: a folded page from a magazine. It crinkled a little when I opened it, but I couldn't resist. I'd never known Vea to read magazines or anything else for that matter.

It was an article from a magazine called *Home & Garden*. "An Oasis for Your Yard," it said. There were lots of pictures of plants and flowers and fountains. It certainly didn't look anything like the Tower.

The article went back into the shoebox, too.

I thought about how I planned to destroy Vea's plants.

I was glad I didn't.

⌘ ⌘ ⌘

It was the cabinets that awakened the Witch Head.

I'd been frightened of the kitchen cabinets the most, because that's where rats, mice, and cockroaches hide when all the lights are out. Every time I opened a cabinet, I expected something to leap out and attack me, so I wasn't able to relax enough to be stealthy. When I opened the third cabinet, something tickled my nose—who knows what—and it startled me. I instinctively slammed the cabinet shut. It closed with a loud WHACK! and I stood there without moving, still following Manny's rules, until I heard Vea's bedroom door open and she appeared, her hair a mess and her eyes squinty. She was cursing under her breath in Cebuano.

"What are you doing?" she said, coughing.

I whipped around, still swiping at my nose. That's when I realized it had probably been a strand of my own hair—not a spider.

"Uh," I said. "Looking for something to eat."

"You don't need anything to eat in the middle of the night, *kano*. Only pigs eat at this hour." She nodded in the direction of the hallway. "Go to bed."

I wasn't in a position to argue. My heart was thundering a million miles a minute. So I headed for the door. But something stopped me before I passed her. It was the look in her eyes. There's something about the early-early morning that makes things look different, even evil Witch Heads like Vea.

"What?" she said, her eyes still squinty.

I suddenly had the urge to ask her something. Anything. *Do you miss your family? Are they all mean like you? Do they have cruel eyes? Why haven't you left us behind or sent us back? Why did you keep that article from that magazine? What was your favorite halo-halo flavor?* But when I opened my mouth, nothing came out.

"What?" she said again. She reached out and plucked the skin on my forehead, hard. I winced. My eyes watered. "You live in your head too much," she said. "Time to wake up." She snapped her fingers in my face. "Daydreams killed your mother, you know."

I just wanted to go back to bed. Back to Ming.

"Good night, Vea," I said, and returned to my room.

❧ 29 ❧
June 2

I don't know how long I slept, but it felt like five minutes. When morning came, I had the feeling that I was falling down a giant hole. But not just my body, my heart, too. It's the feeling you get when you know something bad is about to happen but there's nothing you can do about it. I have the same feeling just before Manny and I take pops from the freezer at Tippet's. It's like having all your insides tumble down and empty out through your toes, only no one can tell because you look normal on the outside.

When I opened my eyes and saw the ceiling, it was like waking up inside the mouth of a whale. Inside it was just me and Ming. Outside was a world where there was no Auntie Jove, no mother, no father, no Amelia. And Ming would find out soon enough because tomorrow—*tomorrow*—was the day.

I wished everything would stop at that moment, with Ming breathing softly in her sleep and dreaming of a place better than here. I wished I was Father Time and could stop the clock.

Ming stirred.

"Sol?" she whispered. Her voice was tired and small.

"Yeah?"

"What's the date today?"

"Novembery thirty-second. We traveled into the future in our sleep and the world uses a different calendar now. All the months have changed. All the cars fly. Once you wake up, we'll put on our jet packs and go to Mars."

She sighed. "Can't you ever be serious? What's the date, *really*? Is it June second?"

No, no. I wanted it to be Novembery thirty-second in a world where Amelia was still alive and my mother still sailed a magic boat.

Daydreams killed your mother, you know.

"Yes," I replied. "It's June second."

"That's what I thought." Ming yawned. "I want to sleep all day until it's June third."

"I want to sleep until the end of time."

A bird chirped outside.

"You haven't packed anything," Ming said.

"I know."

"Don't you want to take something when Auntie Jove comes tomorrow?"

"No."

"Why not?"

"Because."

"What if you need something after we leave?"

"I don't have anything worth taking."

"What about your bracelet?"

I stared at the ceiling. I thought about Mrs. Yeung and her picture.

"Ming?" I said.

"Yeah?"

"What are you going to do if Auntie Jove doesn't show up?"

"She will."

"But what if?"

"She will."

I rolled over, away from her, and brought the covers to my chin. I thought about the family in Blackbeard's glass bottle. The family with their painted-on smiles. I wondered again how Blackbeard got them in there. Maybe he could put me in there, too.

Ming was still asleep at noon, when I went outside to meet Manny and Caroline. They were across the street, facing the Tower, sitting on the curb. The mound of tires and tall grass loomed behind them. It was a gray day, with only a hint of sun.

"You never told us what happened with Blackbeard," said Manny as I crossed the street.

Caroline moved over so I could sit between them.

"Did you have to fight him off as you got away?" Caroline asked, her eyes wide with worry. The rims were really red.

"No, nothing like that," I said. "He wasn't that bad, actually. He was gonna call the police, but then I struck a deal with him."

"What kind of deal?" Manny asked.

I stared straight ahead, at my building. I wondered what it looked like to Caroline, who was so used to seeing houses with white columns and sparkling cars. There was nothing sparkling about Magnolia Tower. The door opened and Mrs. Yeung came out. She was wearing all white linen and an oversized straw hat that shaded her face. She walked off down the street, toward Tippet's. I wondered if she saw me.

I turned one of the pearls on my bracelet between my fingers.

"He said all I have to do is bring him something good to put in his junkyard and he'll forget the whole thing," I said.

Mrs. Yeung walked fast for an old woman.

I wondered how old she was.

"Did he say how much it had to be worth?" asked Caroline.

"Nope. He just said to bring him something."

Manny leaned forward and rested his elbows on his knees. "What're you gonna bring?"

"I don't know," I said. "I don't have anything. Except this." I shook my bracelet. I could barely handle the thought of giving it away. It certainly wasn't junk. Not to me.

"Nah," said Manny. He put his hand over the bracelet and smiled at me. A nice smile. Not his usual idiotic, I'm-being-a-total-pest smile. "You keep it. We'll find something else."

"Hey, maybe we could bring him some tires." Caroline pointed over her shoulder.

"Yeah, he's only got fifty million of 'em," said Manny.

"I could bring you something from my house, Sol," Caroline said. "We have all kinds of stuff in the garage and my mom's always saying it's all junk."

"Really?" Manny leaned forward to look at her, suddenly very interested. "What kind of stuff you got in there? Anything for a certain sexy Mexican boy?"

"Yeah. You know any?"

"Ha!" Manny said. "You're real funny, you know that?"

There was a softer tone in his voice. Maybe he was starting to warm up to her. "I don't want you to bring anything from your house. I'll think of something," I said. "Maybe I'll trade in Vea."

I imagined carrying her there in a wheelbarrow, walking up to Blackbeard and saying, *Here's my junk, sir! Now will you tell me how you got that family in the bottle?*

"What're you doing today?" I asked.

"I thought we were gonna hang out," Manny said. "The three of us."

I shook my head. "I've gotta look after Ming."

"So, bring her along. We can take her to eat hot dogs or heist cars."

"We should walk to my house and introduce her to Constance," Caroline said. Her face was all lit up, like it was the greatest idea ever.

Maybe it was.

Manny scrunched his nose. "Who's *Constance*?"

"My sister," Caroline said. "She's the same age as Ming, and she doesn't have any friends."

"Maybe because her name's *Constance*."

I nudged him. "Shut up, doofus."

Caroline raised her white eyebrows at me. "Well? What do you think?"

I thought of what Ming said to me the other day. *You have Manny and I have Auntie Jove.*

"I think that's the greatest idea ever," I said.

❧ 30 ❧
Steamboat

Things I know to be true: There's a hot dog stand about a block up from Tippet's. Manny and I never eat there because he says hot dogs are made out of pig butts. But you don't have many choices when there are five people and you only have seven dollars total, so Manny, Caroline, and I took Ming and Constance to the Steamboat Hot Dog Stand. Along the way, they challenged each other not to touch any of the cracks in the sidewalk, not to blink, not to talk with their mouths open, and not swing their arms when they walked.

We sat at an outdoor picnic table. Manny, Caroline, and I ordered a big plate of fries. Ming ordered a plain hot dog with ketchup and Constance got the opposite of plain—she had a chili dog with mustard, ketchup, and onions. I've never understood how anyone could eat chili when it's so hot and muggy outside, but Constance didn't seem to care.

"I play the cello," she said, out of the blue. She licked a glob of chili off her chin with her tongue. The girl ate like she'd never eaten before.

"What's the cello?" Ming asked. She'd barely touched her hot dog.

"It's a musical instrument, *duh*. It's, like, this tall." She showed how tall it was, which seemed to be taller than her. "It's kinda like a violin except way better."

"I like to draw," said Ming. She picked up her hot dog with both hands and took a bite, careful not to drop any ketchup anywhere.

"Can you draw me something? Like a unicorn? I love unicorns. I'm, like, *obsessed* with them."

"I don't have a pen or paper."

"That's okay." Constance shrugged and took another enormous bite of her chili dog. A fresh glob splattered on the picnic table. With her mouth full, she added, "You can draw it tonight and give it to me tomorrow."

"I can't. I won't be here tomorrow. Me and my sister are going to live with my aunt in the jungle."

Manny and Caroline both turned to me.

Somewhere down the street, a car horn honked.

"That's okay," Constance said. "You can mail it to me. I'll give you my address."

"I didn't know you had an aunt in the jungle," Manny said, giving me a what's-wrong-with-your-sister look.

"We do," Ming said. She tucked her hands under her legs. The barely touched ketchup-only hot dog sat in front of her. "Her name is Jovelyn, but everyone calls her Jove. Auntie Jove."

"Auntie Jove?" Manny repeated. I knew he'd never heard her name before. I'd never told him any of my mother's stories.

Caroline turned to Ming. "Does she live in the Philippines?"

"She lives everywhere," Ming said.

Constance finished off her chili dog. "You can't live *everywhere*. You can only live in one place at a time."

"Auntie Jove can do anything."

"There are snakes in the jungle," Constance added. "So be sure to wear shoes and socks."

"I will."

"And don't forget to mail my unicorn picture."

"I won't forget," Ming promised. "I never forget."

A faraway sound grew in the distance behind me. *Grr-thump, grr-thump.*

Manny was sitting across from me. He looked over my shoulder. "Ugh. It's that freak girl and boy from the Snout."

Sure enough, Rory and Aiden rolled up alongside the Steamboat, squinting at us. Rory's hair was bright red this time, and they were both on skateboards. I didn't know Rory knew how to skate, too. I figured they'd just keep going—what business would they have with us?—but then they both dropped one sneaker to the cement and came to a stop.

"Hey, Rory and Aiden!" Caroline said, like she was a one-person welcoming committee. "Do you guys wanna eat hot dogs with us?"

"No," Aiden said, flatly.

"We just wanted to find out what you said to that dirty old junk-heap man," Rory said.

"What dirty old junk-heap man?" asked Manny, as if there was more than one.

"You know. The one with the dog," Rory said.

Manny leaned back in his chair and crossed his arms defensively. But it was hard to look menacing with Constance licking chili off her fingers next to him.

"What about him?" Manny asked.

Rory ignored him and looked at me. "He let his dog off the chain."

"Well, hall-lay-lu-yah!" Manny said, shaking his hands in the air. "Life can go on! The Beast is now free to rip our arms off in broad daylight!" He brought his palms together and bowed. "Thank you, thank you. I feel so much safer knowing that we might have our noses eaten off in our sleep."

Ming's eyes were perfect, worried circles.

"Don't worry," Rory said to her. "He's exaggerating because he's an idiot."

Caroline and Constance laughed. And I did, too—a little.

Ming's shoulders relaxed.

"Do either of you want some fries?" Caroline asked Rory, motioning toward our half-eaten order.

"No way," said Aiden. He rolled his skateboard back and forth with the foot he had planted on top of it.

"We never eat here," Rory said. "I'm pretty sure

this place needs to be condemned by the health department."

Ming's eyes widened again.

Manny snorted. "So you're too good for this place or something?"

"Basically," Rory said.

"We don't like puking our guts out over a few hot dogs," Aiden added.

I thought about that time Vea took me to the clinic. If Rory was right and Ming got sick from condemned hot dogs, at least I knew where to bring her.

"Anyway," Rory continued, looking at me. "I have a feeling you had something to do with it, so thanks. And now we don't have to call the ASPCA or break in or anything."

"Yeah," Aiden mumbled. "Thanks."

"No problem," I said.

Constance raised her hand like she was in school, then pointed to Aiden's skateboard. "Do you ever fall off that thing and crack your heads open?"

"Sometimes we fall," said Aiden.

"But we don't crack our heads open, exactly," Rory added.

"Maybe you could teach me how to ride one, because my mom says they're too dangerous," Constance said. "And you can teach my best friend, too." She pointed to Ming, who didn't argue.

"Yeah, maybe," Rory said.

"If she doesn't move to the jungle," Constance added.

"All right," Rory said. "If she doesn't move to the jungle."

Rory gave one slight wave—mostly toward me and Ming—before she and Aiden drifted away, back down the sidewalk.

✖ 31 ✖
June 3

Here are the things Ming packed in her suitcase:

Five of her favorite shirts.

Two pairs of shorts, one of which had a torn pocket.

Two pieces of artwork she made in school, both of which earned a *Fantastic!* smiley sticker from Miss Paulsen. One of the pieces is a rainbow with a pot of gold at the end. The other is a bright blue house with a red door.

Her favorite pen.

The letter box with the broken lock, which she never asked about.

One pair of sandals.

Six pairs of underwear, but only the ones with daisies, because those are her favorite.

Three pieces of bubblegum from Tippet's.

A school notebook, which she will use to "record her adventures."

The suitcase was locked and sitting next to the bedroom door. The sun had just risen, but Ming was fully dressed and so was I, because she insisted. Once she had checked and double-checked her suitcase, she sat on the bed. Her legs bounced up and down like crazy.

"Open the door a little so we can hear when she knocks," she said.

I did. Then I leaned near the doorframe and watched her bouncy knees.

"Ming," I said. "If she doesn't come—"

"She will," Ming said quickly. "Not long after sunrise."

"I know, but if she doesn't—if for some reason, she doesn't—I'll take you for ice cream, okay? Or anything. We can do whatever you want. Just me and you, for the rest of the day."

"Okay. But she will."

"It's always good to have a backup plan. So ice cream will be our first backup plan, and then we'll figure something else out."

She swung her hair over her shoulder and braided it nervously, ignoring my last comment. "What if she doesn't know which apartment building is ours?"

"Ming—"

"We should wait outside. That would be better." She jumped off the bed.

"You can't go outside with that, Ming," I said. "When Vea wakes up, she's going to wonder what you're up to. She'll probably think you're running away."

"Who cares? Auntie Jove will be here soon and it won't matter."

She wrapped her tiny hands over the handle, tried to lift it, and huffed.

"It's too heavy. Will you carry it for me?"

It wasn't heavy at all. Once we were outside, Ming asked me to put it down on the sidewalk near the curb, so I did.

Ming sat on top of her suitcase as if it were a booster seat.

"Auntie Jove is going to think that it's weird you didn't pack anything," she said.

I sat on the curb and looked down the street. It was the same old street as always. Same old Giverny, south of Tippet's.

"What kind of car is she supposedly driving?" I asked.

"I don't know. Why would I ask that?"

"The sun is up now."

"I know. But that doesn't mean anything. People aren't always exactly on time, you know."

The brightness on Ming's face didn't start to fade

until around nine o'clock. The sun had been up for hours by then, but Ming hadn't moved from her spot on her suitcase, not even to go to the bathroom, and she hadn't said a word since just before I went back inside to get us some water, and that was at eight-thirty. Vea was still asleep.

"It's nine o'clock," I said.

"I know."

"You said not long after sunrise, right?"

"She'll be here."

The street was awake now. Someone started a lawn mower. Dogs barked. Cars went by, booming music. A few neighborhood kids blazed past us on their bikes.

"Let's go get that ice cream," I said. "Or we can get hot dogs again."

"No. I'm not moving. What if she comes while we're gone?"

"Vea will be up soon. You don't want her to catch you outside sitting on that suitcase."

By the time Vea decided to look for us, it was almost noon. I'd been thinking about a thousand different things—my hunger, Ming, the sailboat, the heat, Caroline, Mrs. Yeung, Manny—when Vea suddenly appeared behind us, casting a shadow over the scorching cement.

"Hey," she said, but not a greeting. A growl. "What's going on out here?"

I turned to face her. Ming didn't.

I stood up. "Nothing. We're playing a game."

"What kind of game?"

"None of your business."

Vea kicked the suitcase with the toe of her slipper. That jostled Ming. She slammed both of her hands down to keep the suitcase steady and whipped her head around to give Vea the coldest stare I'd ever seen.

Vea laughed. "Someone is getting a little bite in their bark finally, eh?"

"We're just playing a game," I said. "We're pretending we're going on a trip."

"Doesn't look like pretend to me." Vea toed the suitcase again.

"That's because it isn't," said Ming.

My heart dropped.

Of all times for Ming to speak back to Vea, she picked now.

The worst time of all.

I could see the whole thing playing out in my head before it happened, and then it did, just as I pictured:

"Auntie Jove is coming for us," said Ming. "She's going to take us away from you and we're going to be rich and live a happy life without your dirty slippers and stinky smoke."

Vea was silent for a second. Then she threw her head back and laughed—a real, honest, laugh. Between her howls, she said, "Auntie Jove is—what? Oh! That certainly *is* pretend, little mouse! That *is* make-believe!"

"It's not!" said Ming. "It's true! She *is* coming!"

"Auntie Jove? Mei-Mei's made-up 'secret sister,'

Auntie Jove? Yes, I've heard of her. The one who traveled in an elephant parade, yes?" Vea laughed and laughed.

"Don't you ever say my mother's name!" I screamed.

That silenced her. In fact, it silenced the whole street. Even the birds shut up. I couldn't hear the lawn mower anymore, or the booming cars. It was just me, Ming, Vea, and the suitcase.

Vea stuck her finger in my face. "I'll say whatever I choose." Her hair brushed the hollows of her cheeks as she looked down at Ming. "*Ay sus*, you're a stupid little mouse. There is no Auntie Jove, don't you know that? Hasn't your great big *kano* sister told you? No one is coming for you. Your mother made up a sister because she knew her life was boring and useless. She lied to you every day of your lives. I'm the only one who will ever tell you the truth, little mouse. Do you hear me? Don't turn away from me. I'm your only mother now."

In two quick motions, Vea squatted down, grabbed the handle of Ming's suitcase, and pulled it out from under her. Ming fell hard onto the curb and wailed.

Some boys down the street laughed.

"I'm taking this to the same place I took that dirty toy—to the Dumpster, so it can rot with the trash," said Vea.

Ming expected to spend the afternoon of June third settling into a new life with her new beloved auntie, but instead she spent it lying on her belly, in bed, with her big sister holding a bag of ice on her bruised tailbone.

By four o'clock, the bag of ice was forgotten in the bathroom sink and that wail was the last noise Ming had made.

I brushed her hair. I brought her water that she didn't drink. I made a sandwich that she didn't eat.

At five o'clock Vea came into our room.

"You're both punished for the next week. You may not go outside to play. You may not go outside at all." With each sentence, her voice raised higher and higher: "You'll stay right here, in this apartment, and do chores! Do you understand! And if I hear a single complaint, you'll be sorry! Believe me! In fact, don't come out of this room for the rest of the night unless you want your noses twisted off your face!"

She didn't wait for a response, not that she would have gotten one. She slammed the door shut so hard that the doorframe rattled.

I stroked Ming's hair and whispered, "We've been officially kidnapped, little sister."

Then I looked to the corner of the room and said, loudly: "Amelia? Amelia? Where are you?" I'd never talked to Amelia in front of anyone else before. Talking to her was like saying secret prayers. But I didn't care if Ming heard me now. Maybe I wanted her to hear. "You said everyone can do something. What can I do, Amelia? What can I do?"

I waited for the pale white of her skin to appear out of the darkness. I waited for her to tell me things like *I believe in the truth* or *Everyone can do something* or *You've made a fine mess of things, Sol.* I waited for her to talk to me about palace doors and Salvatore the Sitaw Man. But she didn't appear.

She had left me, too.

❊ 32 ❊

The Land of Forgotten Girls

Neither of us slept. Ming's head was on my chest. She was quiet and blinking and breathing softly. She didn't cry. I wished she would. I wished with all my might that she would, because at least that would be something. Instead, she lay there. She hadn't eaten. She had faint black circles under her eyes. I wondered if I had them, too.

I didn't know what time it was, but I could tell it was near dawn. Vea wasn't awake yet, and the apartment building was quiet.

I got out of bed. When I moved, Ming slipped off me and onto the pillow, like a rag doll. I lifted her up so that her head rested on my shoulder and both of her skinny arms wrapped around my neck. She was so light that I was able to hold on to her with one arm. I used the other hand to pick up Vea's nicest plant on the way out—the one with the thick, shiny leaves that looked like miniature umbrellas. Blackbeard had said to bring him something good, after all, and he didn't have any plants like that in his junkyard. I'd never noticed any, at least. But by the time we got to the hallway, where the bulb was out and the light was dim, my muscles ached.

"Ming, you'll have to walk for me, okay? I can't carry everything," I said. I put her down, half expecting her to crumble to the stained carpet, but she put both feet on the ground. "When we walk out those doors, it'll be just the beginning. We will be sister princesses on a fantastic journey to deliver this enchanted plant. Are you ready?" She didn't answer, but she followed me outside, into the early morning air.

The sun was rising. The sky was a mix of red, purple, and blue.

"Look at the sky, Ming," I said as we walked down the stoop. "It's all different colors. If you think hard enough, you can become part of them. Try it. You'll see. Imagine that you're purple or red or blue."

We walked together toward the sidewalk. I lifted Vea's plant toward the field across the street. "You see that?" I said. "That's Tire Mountain. Every night the Goodyear Emperor rises up from there and keeps watch on the field. Sometimes the tires turn into his foot soldiers and they roll in a straight line right down the street. But it's morning now, so they're all asleep."

We moved like sleepwalkers. We were both so tired, so sad, and so strange out there in the dawn. I couldn't remember the last time I'd ever been outside at this hour, if ever. There's something magical about it, but scary. It was like anything could happen at any moment—good or bad, you couldn't tell.

When the free clinic came into view, I pointed that out, too.

"See that place, Ming? That's where they keep spirit birds. You can tell by the picture on the sign. Do you know what spirit birds are?" She didn't answer. Didn't even look. "You tell them your wishes and they fly them up to the clouds. That's why he's got a little leaf in his mouth. He's getting ready to deliver someone's wish." I waved to the dove. "Good luck, spirit bird! Fly safely!" I looked down at Ming. "Do you want to wish him good luck, too?" But she wasn't paying attention. She was staring straight ahead and keeping her pace like a zombie.

To our left was the flimsy tree that Manny had made fun of the other day. *And what tree are you gonna put it in? This one?*

"That tree over there isn't really in bad shape, like you'd think. It's actually a phoenix. Do you know what a phoenix is?" Of course, Ming said nothing. "A phoenix loses all its feathers and gets really, really scrawny and weak. Just when you think that's it for the phoenix, it turns to ashes and rises again. Like a rebirth. And it's bigger and stronger than ever."

The air was starting to get hot and sticky. The sky had turned a deeper shade of pink and purple.

"We're about to reach a critical point on our journey, Sister Princess. Up ahead there's a crack in the sidewalk. A really big crack. You've probably seen it before. But what you don't know is why it's there. It was created by the evil Molten Prince. He's trapped in the center of the earth, and it's very hot, so he's desperate to get out. But that's not the only reason. He also wants to defeat the Bottle King. Have you ever heard of him?" Nothing. "Well, the Bottle King is this man with a very thick beard who has the power to bottle up people's happiest memories and keep them safe. That way people can be happy anytime they want. All they have to do is take the bottle from the shelf and they can relive every happy moment they ever experienced. That's why the Molten Prince tries to crash through the earth, so he can steal all the happy thoughts and keep them for himself. So far he hasn't been able to. Be sure to look out when we get to the crack. Be very, very careful. If you even get one drop of molten lava on your shoe, it'll melt your feet off. Plus we don't want anything to happen to this plant. We're going to offer it to the Bottle King as a trade, so he'll give us something from his magical garden."

When we reached the pyramid crack, I stepped back and hesitated, like I expected fountains of lava to spew out of it. But Ming just kept going. She walked right over it.

I took quick steps to catch up with her.

"The Bottle King will only help you if you give him a gift and your heart is kind. I have the gift—that's why I've got this plant—and you have the heart." We had reached the field. Up ahead and far off the road was the chain-link fence surrounding Blackbeard's junkyard. "He's going to tell us his bottling secret in exchange for this plant. But I'm hoping he'll give us something even better than that: a magic boat for us to sail to the Land of Forgotten Girls."

When we reached the chain-link fence, Ming followed me silently to the main gate. I'd never gone through a legitimate entrance to the junkyard before, but this time I planned to walk right up to the camper, knock on the door, and offer Blackbeard the plant.

Unfortunately, the side gate was locked.

I wondered what time a junkyard was supposed to open.

"This is the Bottle King's magic garden," I said to Ming. "But he's not here yet, so we'll have to—"

I stopped mid-sentence.

Two oddities struck me at the same time. First, the Beast wasn't chained outside anymore—just like Rory said. Second, the old boat. It was leaning against the camper. Restored. Sanded. Painted.

"Wait here, Ming," I said, surprised at the excited pitch of my voice. "I'll be right back."

Still holding Vea's plant, I ran to the hole in the fence and slipped inside. The junkyard had a weird vibe at this hour, like it really was a magical garden, only it was hard to tell if it was enchanted or under a curse.

I weaved around Blackbeard's neighborhoods of motors and chairs and walked up to the rickety steps of the camper. I heard movement on the other side of the disjointed door—the Beast, no doubt, enjoying his new freedom. I hoped he didn't knock down any of Blackbeard's bottles.

I put Vea's plant on the top step—it looked very strange sitting there, with its bright green leaves— then I rounded the camper and saw the boat up close. Ming was on the other side of the padlocked gate with her head resting against the fencepost. She might as well have been on another planet, or another universe. Maybe she was.

The boat was heavier than I expected, but once I got it down on the ground, I was able to pull it behind me like a wagon. It wasn't easy, though. Sometimes I pulled it behind me. Sometimes I pulled it while walking backward. There was so much junk everywhere. I had to pull it around the ratty restaurant booths, chairs and chairs and more chairs, rusty engines, old street signs, and who knows what else. By the time I made it to the hole in the fence, my shirt clung to my back and sweat dribbled into my eyes.

Then there was the business of getting the boat *through* the fence itself.

It would have been a thousand times more helpful if someone was on the opposite side to take the other end, but there was only the open field and the slant of rising sunlight. I managed, though. I propped one end onto the hole, then I squatted down, lifted with all my might, and pushed. It only took two hard shoves. Maybe I was stronger than I thought.

Ming saw me pulling the rowboat—at least I think she did—but she didn't lift her head. So once I had the boat sitting in the middle of the field, facing the rising sun, I went back to her, picked her up, and carried her to it.

There were two boards to sit on. They looked brand-new—nothing like the mess Caroline had discovered. No more rotted wood or cracked slats. They had been sanded and painted, maybe replaced altogether, I wasn't sure. It was definitely way better than anything Manny or I could have done. But Ming didn't seem interested in sitting or doing anything else, so I laid her down in the back of the boat. She leaned her head against the edge. Her black hair spilled over the side.

I sat on the board, facing her.

Blackbeard had sanded down every edge and corner. He'd painted everything a hazy shade of blue. I couldn't imagine him picking that color. He must have chosen it for Ming.

"Are you ready to go to the Land of Forgotten Girls?" I said.

Ming didn't answer.

"Oh! I almost forgot," I continued. I unclasped Mrs. Yeung's bracelet from my arm and put it on Ming's instead. Her wrist was so small that she could've slid the bracelet all the way up to her shoulder if she wanted to. "These are your magic emeralds, so Mother Hush recognizes you."

Ming didn't even look at me. Instead, she closed her eyes—but not as if she was imagining.

She was going to sleep.

Good, I thought. *Good*.

Once I was certain she was sleeping, I curled my body into a tight ball and cried.

When I saw a shape appear across the field, moving slowly, I thought it was my mama. Maybe because I was tired. Maybe because I'd cried until my eyes hurt. Whatever it was, I thought it was her. I thought:

She isn't dead after all! They'd made a mistake and now she's coming back for us! For a half second, everything was perfect.

It wasn't my mother, of course. And it wasn't Auntie Jove. It was Mrs. Yeung. She was carrying something small under her arm. I wondered if it was a puppy, then wondered why Mrs. Yeung would go to the junkyard with a puppy and why she would go to the junkyard at all. I shifted in my seat, embarrassed by the boat and my swollen eyes. I felt so stupid—and Mrs. Yeung would see how stupid I was, too. I actually thought I could do something, but all I'd done was put my little sister in a boat from a junkyard.

She wasn't holding a puppy. It was a stuffed animal. A hippopotamus, the same size as Mr. Elephant.

When Mrs. Yeung reached the boat, she leaned over, lifted Ming into her bony arms with one swift movement, and said, "Come."

❈ 33 ❈
Mother Hush

When I was little and didn't want to help my mother with the housework, she would tell me the story of Rip Van Winkle. She said he was lazy and all he ever wanted to do was sleep. One day he fell asleep under a tree and didn't wake up for twenty years. When he opened his eyes and blinked, everything in his village was different. His children were all grown up. A war had been fought and won. And he didn't know anyone. Even his dog was gone.

I don't remember following Mrs. Yeung
back to Magnolia Tower and I don't remember
changing from my dirty clothes to soft pajamas
and crawling into a bed of fresh linen, but I must
have, because I woke up in an unfamiliar room.
My head pounded like I'd been asleep for twenty
years. And, just like Rip Van Winkle, everything
was different.

There was a table next to the bed with a lamp.
There were framed, black-and-white pictures on the
wall, like the one Mrs. Yeung had shown me before.
Mrs. Yeung's family, I guess. They smiled back at me
like peaceful ghosts from the past. The room smelled
like books and tea.

I slipped out of bed and my feet sank into a thick,
plush rug. The carpets here weren't dusted with ash.
The rug was light purple, the color of lilac, same as
the lamp on the table.

Where was Ming?

I was happy not to wake up in apartment four,

but it still felt weird to be here, wearing old-lady cotton pajamas with a ruffled collar.

In the hallway, I confirmed what I already knew: I was in Mrs. Yeung's apartment. I saw the couch, her stacks of books, and heard the clinking of teacups. I could even see the back of Mrs. Yeung's head, charcoal-black with streaks of gray. I approached slowly. That's when I saw Ming. She was asleep on the couch with her head on Mrs. Yeung's lap and the hippopotamus in the crook of her arm. I was happy I'd woken up first so she could see me when she opened her eyes. If Ming saw Mrs. Yeung first, she'd be scared.

Mrs. Yeung sipped her tea as if having a sick little girl who she'd never really met asleep on her couch was the most natural thing in the world.

"Mrs. Yeung?" I said.

She looked up. Didn't smile exactly, but looked at me with those kind eyes.

"I didn't know you spoke English," I said.

She spaced her index finger and thumb less than an inch apart.

"Little bit," she said.

I sat on the other end of the couch and put Ming's feet on my lap. The only sound then was Mrs. Yeung's small sips of tea, and the *tink* of the teacup when she set it on the coffee table. Then it was silent. I thought about the restored boat and what Blackbeard would think when he saw it in the grass. I'd go back for it, but not today. Maybe tomorrow.

I'm not sure how long Mrs. Yeung and I sat there—maybe ten minutes, maybe an hour—before Ming woke up. Her eyes suddenly fluttered open and focused on the soft folds of Mrs. Yeung's face. Mrs. Yeung looked down at her.

Ming blinked and blinked. She didn't look for me. She didn't cry out. She didn't close her eyes and fall back asleep, or ask where she was or how she got there.

Instead, she said, "Are you Mother Hush?"

"*Shì*," said Mrs. Yeung.

"Have you come to rescue us?"

"*Shì*."

We didn't have to ask what *shì* meant.

❧ 34 ❧

Captain Horatio

Things I know to be true: Cartoons make good background noise. There are always fun things happening: strange sounds like *zing*s and *ding*s and *splat*s and *zoom*s; people getting run over or hit on the head, but never hurt; goofy voices that you never hear in real life. There are things to laugh at or about, all the time. When you're sick, cartoons are as good as medicine, that's what I think. Even Manny agrees. Last year we watched

Adventure Time practically all summer while Vea was at work.

Some people might think twelve is too old for cartoons, but I think you can watch them whenever you want. I guess Mrs. Yeung felt the same way, because after Ming woke up she put on *Captain Horatio* and turned the volume way up. Mrs. Yeung's eyes narrowed and she squinted at the screen, like she was concentrating really hard, but she laughed when funny things happened and Ming did, too. Cartoons don't care what language you speak.

Ming gave her own commentary.

"Horatio's going to fall in the hole!" she said, pointing at the TV and looking at Mrs. Yeung. "Oh, no, now he's gonna get splattered!"

Each time Ming laughed, she scooted closer to Mrs. Yeung until she was halfway on her lap. Mrs. Yeung didn't seem to mind.

If you didn't know any better, you'd think we were two well-loved girls on a visit with our grandmother. You might think that after cartoons we would bake cookies and tell stories before going home to our parents. You might think we'd be back at Christmastime to open a thousand gifts under the glow of green and red lights, and that we'd hang popcorn strings and sing Christmas carols.

But life has a way of reminding you what is and isn't the truth.

The knocks came in quick succession on Mrs. Yeung's door, and I knew right away it was Vea. *Knockknockknockknockknock.* We could hear it clearly over the sound of Captain Horatio shooting off in a rocket to the moon.

Mrs. Yeung stood up slowly. She opened the door without hesitation.

Ming and her hippopotamus scurried over to me.

"Where are my girls?" asked Vea. I could smell the cigarette smoke from where I sat. She was just like a dragon.

Mrs. Yeung nodded over her shoulder toward us.

Captain Horatio's voice cut through the silence: *Oh, no, Officer Zillah! This isn't the moon at all!*

"It's time for them to come home," said Vea.

No one moved.

Ming scooted closer. Her hair smelled like sweat and bubblegum.

"I don't want to go, Sir Hippo," Ming whispered to the hippopotamus. "I want to stay with Mother Hush."

"Give me my girls," said Vea. "Or I'll call the police."

Mrs. Yeung reached into her pocket and pulled out a phone. I didn't even know she carried a phone. She held it out to Vea like a slice of cake.

I don't know where we are, Captain Horatio, but the ground tastes delicious!

"I don't want to go," Ming whispered again.

Vea leaned against the doorframe. It shifted under her shoulder. She blew smoke in Mrs. Yeung's face. Mrs. Yeung didn't move. Not a single muscle.

"Amelia," I whispered, so low that only Ming and

Sir Hippo could hear me. "What can we do, Amelia?"

But she wouldn't answer. I knew she wouldn't.

"No use coming to this country if you can't even speak *English*, you know," Vea said.

Mrs. Yeung raised the phone higher, as if to say *Will you call or will you leave?*

I wondered the same thing. My heart was like a hummingbird again, but I willed it to slow down. I didn't want Ming to feel how fast it was beating.

"You can keep the little devils," Vea said. "It'll give me a nice break and some peace and quiet. All they do is cause trouble, anyway."

She didn't leave. Not right away. But then the ground shifted, the doorframe slipped back into place, and Mrs. Yeung quietly shut the door and returned to the sofa.

Look at the view of earth from here, Officer Zillah! It's so small it could fit on the tip of my thumb.

❧ 35 ❧
Sister Princesses

We couldn't stay with Mrs. Yeung forever. Ming and I both knew that. We went back to apartment four the next day. When we walked through the door, Vea was wearing her Stop-N-Go uniform and pouring uncooked rice into the rice cooker. The television was on—just people yelling at each other.

Mrs. Yeung had washed our clothes, so we were fresh and clean. Our hands smelled like lemons, because Mrs. Yeung had let us shine some of her silver. She paid us twenty dollars apiece and gave us each a polished spoon. I slipped mine in my back pocket. We felt rich. Especially Ming, since she had gotten to wear the hundred-dollar bracelet. She had to give it back to me, though, because it kept falling off.

Vea turned toward us like a lion eyeing its prey.

"Stop right there," she said, before we could go any further. Her voice was low. Probably because she knew Mrs. Yeung might be listening.

I put my hand on Ming's back and gave her a light shove. Ming was clutching Sir Hippo so tightly to her chest that I could see the whites of her knuckles.

"Go to our room," I said.

Ming took two steps, uncertain.

"No, little mouse," Vea said. "You stay right there. I'm the mother here."

Ming stopped. Turned. She looked at me. *What should I do?* her eyes said.

"Go to the room," I said again.

Vea clutched both sides of the rice cooker and took long strides toward us. Her face was shoved up, hard. It was the look of a true dragon. An evil witch head. Vea.

In one swift, angry motion, she tipped the rice cooker forward and hurled the kernels in my face. They hit me like thousands of armored seeds. Let them prick my skin. I didn't flinch.

"Go to our room," I said to Ming, more forcefully. Her eyes glistened with coming tears. I gave her a look that said, *Do as I say*. And she did.

She didn't shut our bedroom door all the way. She kept it open just a crack. She probably didn't realize that I could see her clearly, dark eyes peeking between the door and the frame.

Ming would make a terrible spy.

"You were grounded," said Vea. "You both were. And you left this house. Disobedient." She accentuated every syllable. It made her sound like a snake. Dissssobedient.

"You were a girl once," I said. "You ate bright blue *halo-halo*."

Vea didn't know what to do with that. The look on her face changed. I didn't recognize it.

"If you don't want us, why don't you send us back to the Philippines?" I said. "You could put us in a basket, like Moses. We can find our own way."

Her eyes narrowed. "Clean up this rice and go to your room."

"I will kneel on this rice before I ever clean it."

This amused her. "Oh, really? Go ahead, then. Be my guest. Two minutes and you'll be begging me to let you clean it up."

I knelt.

"You stole my best plant," said Vea, glaring down at me. "You and the little mouse, you're both thieves. What did you do with it, eh? Did you give it to that old woman? What else did you take?"

"Just the plant," I said. "But I didn't give it to Mrs. Yeung. I gave it to the Bottle King."

I tried not to wince. Have you ever knelt on rice? At first it wasn't so bad. It just felt like little hard pellets pushing against my skin. But the longer I knelt, the worse it got.

I kept kneeling, though. Just to show her, once and for all.

"You can't control me," I said, looking up at her. "I'll stay here for hours if I have to."

She leaned on one hip. "Go ahead, *kano*."

"My science teacher taught me about azaleas once," I said. What was I even talking about? I didn't know. Maybe Amelia had taken control of my body. "They're a plant that only blooms once a year. The kids in my class thought it was stupid to have a plant that only blooms once. But I thought it was the best kind of plant. Who cares if you have flowers all year? After a while, it'd get boring. But once a year, that's different."

My knees were tired. My thighs ached. The kernels pushed, pushed, pushed against me like a dozen pinpricks.

"What are you even talking about, *kano*?" Vea said.

"Azaleas. You should get one."

I looked to the bedroom door. Ming was still there, staring out at me and clutching Sir Hippo. I wondered how long she'd stand there—but I didn't have to wonder long. She opened the door and came out. My stomach flipped. She was like a gazelle walking into an open field.

But Vea barely looked at her.

"Sister Princesses don't leave each other," said Ming. She knelt on the rice next to me. "This is Sir Hippo," she said to Vea. "If you hurt him like you hurt Mr. Elephant, I'm going to put *you* in the Dumpster."

"Ha!" Vea said. "Just try, little mouse. Just try."

But you know what?

She didn't twist our noses off our face.

She didn't spit in our hair or kick our feet.

When Ming winced from the rice, Vea said, "Get up from there, both of you."

And then she went to her bedroom and closed the door.

That night, I pushed the chair against the doorknob and we emptied our pockets on the bed. Forty dollars and two pieces of polished silver! Not to mention Sir Hippo. Ming sat on the bed and lifted up his two front legs to make him dance on the headboard. Then she stopped and frowned.

"Do you think Mr. Elephant will be mad that I have Sir Hippo now?" she asked.

I laid across the bed, picked up one of the spoons, and gazed into it. My distorted reflection stared back at me, smiling.

"No."

She stared into Sir Hippo's button eyes, then turned to me.

"Do you think it's my fault Mr. Elephant died?"

I looked up fast. "No. Why would it be your fault?"

"Because I forgot about him. I was thinking about the fancy paper at Tippet's, and I left him on the bed. I didn't take him with me. I forgot."

"No. It's not your fault. How could you know what would happen?"

I thought about Amelia. I remembered my mother calling my name while I hid behind the coconut tree. *It's not your fault, Sol,* my mother had said, after. *It's nobody's fault.*

"Sometimes bad things just happen," I said. I wished I could have said something better or smarter, something more grown up, but that's what came out of my mouth.

It seemed to work. Ming nodded and went back to making Sir Hippo dance.

"Sol?" she said.

I was still thinking about Amelia.

"Yeah?"

"What're we gonna do with all this money?"

"Hide it in the closet. For later."

"What happens later?"

I jumped up.

"Even miracles take a little time, Cinderella. Now—what in the world did I do with that magic wand?" I looked around and around. Ming laughed. "Oh, yes. Here it is." I lifted the polished spoon and pointed it at the bed—*bibbidi-bobbidi-boo*—and the closet—*bibbidi-bobbidi-boo*—and the door and Sir Hippo and Ming herself. I changed the bed into a coach, Sir Hippo into a footman, and Ming into Cinderella.

"What do we do now?" asked Ming, eyes shining. "Wait for a prince?"

"No," I said. "We call Manny."

36

The Favor

We decided to meet at Tippet's the next morning at ten o'clock. I showed up on time—and for the first time ever, so did Manny.

I was sitting on one of the milk crates when he walked up, carrying the plant I'd requested. He was holding it like someone had accidentally attached it to his hand.

"I could've just brought this to the Tower," he said. "I looked like a dork carrying this through the neighborhood."

"You look like a dork anyway," I said, taking the plant. It was heavy. Pretty. Thick, dark leaves, shaped like teardrops. "Besides, I didn't want Vea to see where I got it." I reached into my pocket. "How much?"

"My dad says don't worry about it. Just be sure to follow the directions." He sat on the crate next to me. "Why are you giving that evil witch a present, anyway? She doesn't deserve it."

"It's not a present. It's to replace the one I stole."

He shrugged. "Still."

"So what are the directions?"

"I can't remember them all," Manny said. "Basically azaleas, or whatever you call 'em, are the most irritating plant in the freakin' universe. In the winter you gotta keep it in a certain temperature—I can't remember what it is—and then in the spring or summer or whatever you have to put a certain kinda fertilizer in there and you have to trim the leaves and stuff. I don't know; I wasn't really listening."

"Thanks for that very detailed explanation," I said.

"My dad says she can ask him if she has any trouble."

I tried to imagine Vea on the phone with Manny's dad, chatting about azaleas. It was hard to picture.

"Do you want to get some bomb pops?" I asked. "I have money."

"You mean they charge for those?"

I laughed. "C'mon. It'll be our first legitimate bomb pop of the summer."

We went inside and bought four. And you know what? They tasted the best.

There are certain things you expect to see when you come home, especially if you've been walking through the same door every day for the past zillion years. So when I opened the door of apartment four and heard Vea laughing—not cackling in her evil witch way, but *laughing*—I had to make sure I was at the right place. Sure enough, the "4" was there, hanging sideways like always.

Had I been transported to another universe?

I walked in with the azalea, confused. Hairbun Lang was there, sitting next to Vea on the couch. They both turned to me.

Vea's laugh drifted away, like she'd been caught with her hand in a cookie jar. She leveled her eyes at the plant.

"What's that?" she asked.

I walked over to the window and put the azalea where the umbrella plant used to be.

"I picked it up this morning," I said. I tried to make my voice sound more enthusiastic, but it's not easy to change the way you talk to someone when you've been doing it for so long. "To replace the other one."

June elbowed Vea. I spotted a job application on the couch next to her.

"How nice, to have a daughter that brings you

little gifts," said June. "My daughter is nothing but a pain in the neck, asking me all the time if she can do this or she can do that. I tell her, Why you keep asking when I always say no?"

Vea was still looking at the plant.

"It's an azalea," I said. "There's all these special instructions to take care of them, but I can't remember what they are. They need certain fertilizer and temperatures and stuff."

"There's a garden store uptown that has all those things," said June. "That's where I get my herbs. They'll know what to do."

I didn't say anything else. Instead, I went to find Ming.

❧ 37 ❧

The Truth

On our way to the junkyard, Ming carried Sir Hippo on her shoulders as she pointed out Tire Mountain and told him about the foot soldiers that rolled through the streets at night. Only, Sir Hippo couldn't sit upright so he kept slouching over and landing on top of Ming's head.

"Does Blackbeard really bottle up people's memories?" she asked.

"He's the Bottle King. And yes. You'll see."

"How does he do it?"

"I don't know. That's what I want to find out."

I thought about the painted-on smiles. The sailboat. The genie on the pillows.

We reached the pathetic tree. Ming told Sir Hippo about the phoenix.

We reached the free clinic. She told him about the spirit birds.

When we reached the pyramid crack, Ming balanced on one foot to jump over it.

"Sol?" she said.

I dodged the pyramid, too. "Yeah?"

"Do you think Mother Hush will let us stay over whenever we want?"

"Yes."

"Do you think she'll keep knocking on the door when she hears Vea yelling?"

"Yes."

"Do you think I can eat hot dogs again with Constance?"

"Yes."

"Do you think the hot dogs will make us sick?"

"No."

The sun beat down on my back. My neck warmed. Ming went back to hopping. Sir Hippo bounced along with her.

Birds chirped, sounding just like Manny.

"Sol?" said Ming.

"Yeah?"

"I don't think Mrs. Yeung is Mother Hush. I think she's just Mrs. Yeung."

"Maybe."

"I'll still call her Mother Hush, though. Just for pretend. You think that's okay?"

"*Shì*," I said.

Ming laughed.

The field leading to the junkyard came into view.

"That looks like a junkyard," Ming said to Sir Hippo. "But it's really a magic garden. There are millions of treasures buried in there."

Our boat was sitting in the same spot. Ming took off running and climbed inside.

"Hey, wait for me," I said, but she didn't hear.

I felt light and airy, like a cloud. For some reason, I thought of Salvatore the Sitaw Man. The people all around when my mama told me about him. The way I looked for seeds in his ears every time we bought string beans. I could smell the air of the market and see all the bright, bright colors of eggplant, plantains, guava, mango. I closed my eyes and heard the lilt of Mama's voice from the in-between. When I looked at Ming again, the sky was brighter, warmer, and she was pretending to hoist the sails. The boat seemed to lift from the ground—a blue crescent on a sea of scorched grass—and linger there. Or was it my imagination?

Amelia's voice drifted out of Ming's invisible sails.

The truth has a thousand voices, she said.

❌ ❌ ❌